Healing the Wounded Soul

Healing The Wounded Soul

Ways to Inner Wholeness

volume I

ARLINE WESTMEIER

ReadersMagnet, LLC

Healing the Wounded Soul: Ways to Inner Wholeness—Volume 1
Copyright © 2020 by Arline Westmeier

Published in the United States of America
ISBN Paperback: 978-1-952896-58-3
ISBN eBook: 978-1-952896-57-6

All rights reserved. No part of this publication may be reproduced, stored in a retrieval system or transmitted in any way by any means, electronic, mechanical, photocopy, recording or otherwise without the prior permission of the author except as provided by USA copyright law.

UnlessUnless otherwise indicated, Biblical quotations are taken from the New King James Version (NKJV), copyright © 1982 by The Thomas Nelson Publishers, or The New International Version (NIV), Copyright © 1986 by Holman Bible Publishers.

The opinions expressed by the author are not necessarily those of ReadersMagnet, LLC.

ReadersMagnet, LLC
10620 Treena Street, Suite 230 | San Diego, California, 92131 USA
1.619.354.2643 | www.readersmagnet.com

Book design copyright © 2020 by ReadersMagnet, LLC. All rights reserved.
Cover design by Ericka Obando
Interior design by Rey Alba

*Dedicated to
my late husband,
Karl,
Our children and grandchildren,
David and Ruthie,
Benjamin and Matthew*

Table of Contents

Foreword 9

1 Integral Healing 13
2 The Function of the Mind 25
3 Basic Human Needs 37
4 The Inferiority Complex 55
5 Healing the Identity 65
6 Obstacles to Telling the Truth 87
7 The Occult and the Decision for Christ 99
8 Prayer Guides for Healing 107
9 Remaining Healed 119
10 The Life Ready for Service 135

About the Author 149

Foreword

During the 21 years my husband and I served as missionaries with the Christian and Missionary Alliance in Colombia, South America, we had the privilege of sharing in the lives of many people. After nine years in student ministries and church planting, we began teaching at the Seminario Bíblico Alianza de Colombia, Armenia (now Bogotá).

While serving there as school nurse and clinical counselor, I became more and more awarae of the need to integrate my secular training in psychology with my knowledge of and faith in the living, saving God. So many students had deep traumas which their faith was not resolving. With my secular knowledge I could diagnose their problems, but its methods were too slow to help all of them.

As I searched for a better way, my husband gave me a small pamphlet written by Bishop Uribe-Uribe of Sonsón. There I found the seeds for what I was searching. With this background information the Lord slowly led me into the joyful realization that He had come to heal the psyche as well as the spirit and body.

Since so many students had so many needs, it was impossible to reach all of them on a one to one basis. As a result a seminar began to take shape, first in successive chapel periods and then in surrounding churches. This led in turn to seminars and retreats in many denominations and cities. In the seminary, the workshops were followed with personal counseling. In churches, as many individuals as possible received personal counseling between sessions; the rest were referred to their pastors.

When I began praying with people to help them bring their traumas to Jesus, I was not prepared for the rapidity of their healing. I felt stunned; I could not believe what was happening. People who would normally have taken years to heal were noticeably better within weeks. I was overwhelmed with a new awareness of the love and compassion of God for His wounded children.

At the same time, I grew increasingly aware that this was not a "magic button" one could press to make everything all right. It required real soul searching before the Lord. People needed to be willing to search out and admit the truth of their innermost thoughts and emotions regardless of the cost. Just as they had agreed and confessed that what God said about their sins was true, they now had to agree and confess that what God told them about their traumas and feelings were true. Just as they had taken God through their lives and confessed their sins so that they could be forgiven, they now had to take God through their lives and tell the truth about their psychological pain and emotions so that they could be healed. This can become very frightening, and some people turn away.

I also came to realize that God seems to heal in "layers." He would heal as much as the people could bring to Him; then they needed to grow into that newly reclaimed area of their lives. Later God would bring up a new layer of pain which would awaken new areas in need of healing. Each successive phase of life awakened its own new areas of need, such as dating, marriage, parenting, and so on. This process can take days, weeks, months or even years.

Together with their psychological healing, people also needed to learn how to enter into and live in their new lives of freedom. What happened when they experienced new traumas? If God loved them and healed them, why weren't all their problems resolved? How could they reach out to help others? The frequency of these and similar questions led to the last part of the seminar, where they finally come to realize that God has been with them all through their trials, preparing them for service.

In order to ensure the people's anonymity, all names, identifying data and many places have been changed. All scripture quotations are from the *New International Version* unless otherwise indicated. I thank Joyce Sauder and Louise Maust for their help in preparing the English manuscript.

This book is dedicated to my husband, Karl, and our children, David and Ruthie who have encouraged and prayed for me throughout the years, and to all the people in Latin America, Europe and the U.S.A. who have permitted me to share in their lives.

Arline Westmeier, Ph.D.

CHAPTER I

Integral Healing

"Mama! Quick—close your eyes! There comes a snake! You're going to faint!" Francia had learned how snakes affected her mother.

Esther didn't close her eyes. She watched the whole program about the snake without fainting. "It was then," she told me later, "that I knew I was healed. Only God could have changed me so completely."

Esther was five years old when *La Violencia*[1] (The Violence) reached its worst in Colombia. She had seen her father kneeling with his arms raised, begging the soldiers who surrounded him with drawn rifles not to shoot him and rape the women of the family. Since they had influential family members in the Conservative Party, he was finally allowed to live.

Every week Esther saw mutilated bodies brought by the truckload to be thrown into the chasm close to their house.

---

[1] *La Violencia* was a time (usually dated from 1948 until 1958 and even later) when the two political parties in Colombia, South America began a campaign to exterminate each other.

She could see the buzzards circling overhead awaiting their feast.

Esther vividly remembered the day she and her sister made their daily trek into the chasm for water for household use. As they approached the chasm they saw two men carrying a corpse, tied hands and feet to a pole between them. As the men came nearer, the girls saw that the corpse had no head.

Behind them came another man, carrying the head in a bloodied gunny sack. These and similar scenes were repeated for over two years. Finally, when their buildings were burned to the ground, the family left the farm.

Now, as an adult, Esther lived in terror of the open country—especially of snakes. Even seeing a snake on television made her faint. She hated the people who had made her family suffer so much. This hatred and terror grew until one day she awoke to find herself tied into a bed in a psychiatric hospital. She had been there two months before becoming aware of where she was.

If I had been a man," Esther said, "I would have joined the guerrillas. I wanted to kill those people."

One day someone told Esther that Jesus wanted to change her and she gave herself to him. Her life changed radically. However, her fear of the country and of snakes remained unchanged. The mere mention of guerrilla activities filled her with terror.

After one of my seminars, Esther asked for a personal appointment. In tears she told me the story of her life, trembling with fear as she talked about what had happened during La Violencia. When she had finished, I asked God to open her spiritual eyes to what Jesus would have done if He had been on earth and had come to their farm when all this happened. I urged her to once again remember the scene of her father kneeling with his hands raised, begging the soldiers in a circle around him not to kill him and rape the women.

"Esther," I said, "imagine Jesus coming into that scene. If Jesus would have gone to each of the soldiers and cast all the hate out of every one of them, they would have fallen to their knees one by one (the Bible says that every knee shall bow before Him) and thrown away their guns. See how Jesus would have collected the guns and puts them away. Then Jesus goes to your father and helps him to his feet. He embraces him and takes away his fears. Then Jesus comforts your mother and sister. Then He comes to little Esther, takes her into his strong arms, and quiets her fear and trembling."

"Now, Esther," I continued, "remember the scene of the headless body. In your memory, go back to that chasm with your sister. In your mind's eye, see those two men coming, carrying the headless body tied to the pole. But look! There comes Jesus! (Remember what He did when He saw the widow's son who had died? He brought him back to life!) See how Jesus would have walked up to the two men carrying the body and commanded them to lay it on the ground. Then he tells the man carrying the gunnysack to bring the head and put it at its proper place on the body. Now remember how God restored the dry bones in Ezekiel 37. In your memory, see how Jesus would have restored life into this body. He raises the man back to life and takes away all the terror he felt when he realized he was going to be murdered."

I put my hands gently over Esther's eyes and ears and prayed, "Thank you, Lord, that you wanted to restore that man. Now heal these eyes that have seen and these ears that have heard these terrible things. Heal this mind that has stored these memories. Engrave these new scenes of your presence so deeply into Esther's memory that each time she remembers what happened she will also remember how you would have restored everything with your presence."

Now, several weeks later, when Esther and her daughter saw the snake appear on television, Esther knew that God had brought about a deep healing in her. Snakes had become a symbol of the terror of her childhood. Now even the symbol was losing its terror.

God's Healing

How is it possible that Esther could have been healed so deeply? We must understand that since God made us, He knows us better than we know ourselves. Psychologists who study human beings can learn certain truths about people, but God who created us knows exactly how He made everything that is in us. If something inside us doesn't function correctly, He who made us understands exactly where the problem lies.

The prophet Isaiah (61:1-4) said of Jesus, the coming Messiah:

> The Spirit of the Lord is upon me, because the Lord has anointed me to preach good news to the poor. He has sent me to bind up the broken-hearted, to proclaim freedom for the captives and release from darkness for the prisoners, to proclaim the year of the Lord's favor and the day of vengeance of our God, to comfort all who mourn, and to provide for those who grieve in Zion—to bestow on them the crown of beauty instead of ashes, the oil of gladness instead of mourning, and the garment of peace instead of despair.

They will be called oaks of righteousness, plantings of God for the display of His splendor. They will rebuild the ancient ruins and restore places long devastated; they will renew the ruined cities that have been devastated for generations.

When Jesus quoted this passage at the beginning of His ministry, He added, "Today this scripture is fulfilled in your hearing." (Luke 4:21)

Jesus came to heal the brokenhearted, to give beauty instead of ashes, gladness instead of mourning and praise instead of despair. He came to set the captives free, including those who are taken captive of their own complexes. Jesus came to give us liberty.

Psalm 147:3, the Psalmist says, "He heals the brokenhearted and binds up their wounds." God does not scold us when we are wounded; He comforts and heals us. He has compassion for us. He understands how hurt we feel and longs to make us whole again.

Isaiah 53:4-5 says, "Surely he took up our infirmities and carried our sorrows, yet we considered him stricken by God, smitten by him, and afflicted. But he was pierced for our transgressions, he was crushed for our iniquities; the punishment that brought us peace was upon him, and by his wounds we are healed."

Look at verse four again. "He took our infirmities and carried our sorrows." Infirmities and sorrows are two different things. Infirmities are physical illnesses while sorrows affect us psychologically. Jesus also carried our sins to the cross. Sicknesses, sorrows and sins are all different and affect different parts of our being.

In 1 Thessalonians 5:23-24 Paul writes, "May God himself, the God of peace sanctify you through and through.

May your whole spirit, soul, and body be kept blameless at the coming of our Lord Jesus Christ. The one who calls you is faithful and He will also do it."

In Greek, the language in which the New Testament was originally written, the word which we have translated as soul is *psychi*, from which comes our word "psyche".

If we read the verse in the original language, we have, "And may God Himself, the God of peace sanctify you through and through. May your whole spirit, psyche, and body be kept blameless at the coming of our Lord Jesus Christ. The one who calls you is faithful, and He will also do it."

We can portray these three parts of the human being with a triangle.

<Insert Image 1>

Spiritual Healing

As Christians we hear a great deal about the fact that Jesus came to bring us spiritual healing, which means He came to bring forgiveness for our sins and make peace between us and God. This is the basis for all our healing.

We can illustrate this with the base line of the human triangle shown above.

<Insert Image 2>

When a person gives himself to Jesus, Jesus comes into his life, cleanses him from sin, makes him a child of God, and he is saved. The Greek language uses the word ***sozo***, for both "to save" and "to heal." Jesus did not only come to save us but also to heal us. When He saves us spiritually He also heals the spirit. It is all one process.

Physical Healing

THE BIBLE ALSO SPEAKS OF PHYSICAL healing. James 5:14-15 tells us that if someone is sick he shall call the elders of the church to anoint him with oil and pray for him, so that he will be healed. In Colombia we hear a lot about physical healing. Big campaigns are held with special emphasis on praying for the sick. Although healing our physical illnesses is very important, we will not deal further with that part since that is not the subject of this book.

But we can add the line for physical healing to our human triangle.

<Insert Image 3>

This, however, leaves one part of the human triangle without healing.

Psychological Healing

THE PSYCHE IS A VERY IMPORTANT PART of a person. In spite if this, its healing has rarely been spoken of in our churches. We rarely hear that Jesus came to heal our psyche. This part of our life is usually turned over to a psychologist or psychiatrist. However, Jesus died to heal our psyche just as He did to heal our body and spirit. The complete human triangle appears this way:

<Insert Image 4>

All this is brought about through prayer.

In Colombia much time is spent fasting and praying for spiritual problems, often accompanied with casting out demons. If demons are present, they must be cast out. But sometimes the roots of these problems are not located in the area of the spirit. Sometimes they are found in the psyche, and unless the psychological wounds are healed very little spiritual progress can take place.

Jorge is a young man from whom Christian counselors tried to cast out demons seven times. But Jorge received no relief, because the root of his difficulty was located not in his spirit but in his psyche. He had deep psychological traumas from his relationship with his father. When these painful memories were brought to Jesus for healing, his "demons" also left.

Many Christians believe that when they give their lives to Jesus and are spiritually healed, all of life should be taken care of forever. But soon they learn that certain things from their past still affect them. They feel depressed, and suffer from fears and phobias. They begin to ask themselves, "Isn't my whole past forgiven? Haven't I been made a new creature in Christ Jesus? Isn't everything that happened to me taken care of?"

It is true that everything has been forgiven. But that does not necessarily mean that everything is healed, because we are speaking of two different areas of the person's life. Forgiveness brings us spiritually into a right standing with God, while healing our traumas brings relief from psychological pain.

I use the word "healed" in a relative way. We will never be completely free until we arrive in heaven, because problems are a normal part of living in this world. We may get sick with the common cold and still continue on with our normal routines. But if we get pneumonia or some other sickness that requires us to remain in bed or be hospitalized, we are no longer dealing with "normal" illnesses. We need special medication, rest and prayer for our physical healing.

As long as we are in this life, we will suffer from spiritual trials and temptations or may even fall into sin from which we immediately repent. But if we turn our backs on God and deliberately walk in known sin, we are no longer dealing with the "normal" spiritual conditions of this life. We need to return to God for our spiritual restoration and healing.

In the same way, at times we will feel insecure or depressed, but continue to function normally with no great difficulty. This will continue as long as we are in this life. But if we become so depressed and insecure or have such difficulties understanding others that we can no longer function freely or may even need to be hospitalized, we are no longer dealing with the "normal" ups and downs of life. We need to bring our griefs and sorrows to Jesus for our psychological healing.

Many Christians seem to believe that when they accept Jesus as their Savior, their lives should be filled with constant "glory's" and "hallelujah's." Everything from that point onward should progress in complete perfection. They seem to believe that no true Christian could have psychological difficulties; if they were "spiritual" enough all their problems would disappear.

After one of our seminars, a student told me that was the first time she had ever heard that true Christians could freely admit their psychological difficulties. "I always believed that for a Christian everything had to go well," she said. "One must always be full of joy. Otherwise we would be saying that Jesus was no good." We find this kind of thinking in the following story.

Stella

STELLA WAS ALWAYS SINGING. FROM MORNING to evening, she sang praise and worship choruses. She was always so happy—so much so that I finally concluded she had some deep, hidden sorrow in her life. Sooner or later, every person wakes up with a stomachache or some other malady, or simply doesn't feel like singing. Stella sang every day.

When I learned to know her better I asked her, "Could it be, Stella, that you have a deep, hidden hurt inside of you?"

Stella looked at me for a minute, then dropped her head and murmured, "Yes, *Hermana* (Sister), I have a problem."

When she was six years old, Stella had been raped. This incident, which she called "my problem," made her feel worthless. She wanted to die and begin life again. One day she heard someone preaching in the street who asked, "Do you want to begin a new life?" Stella thought to herself, "That is exactly what I want." That day she gave her life to Jesus and became a child of God.

However, the pain from her past still remained intact. When Stella tried to talk to her spiritual counselor about her problem, she told her, "Don't ever in your life mention that again, because it has been forgiven. Forget about it!"

But try as she would, Stella could not forget the past. The more she tried to forget, the more she remembered it all. Because of this, she sang from morning to night. She was trying to cover her pain with singing.

Together we asked Jesus to walk with Stella through her memories. We cast her pain on Jesus and watched him carry it to the cross. We asked Him to take the little six-year-old girl in Stella's memory into his strong arms and protect her. In this way Stella became free from the pain of her past. She no longer had to sing from morning to evening.

Sometime later she changed jobs and began studying for her high school diploma. Several years passed before I met her again. "How are you doing with your problem?" I asked.

"My problem? What problem? My grades are good. I don't have any problem," she said.

"No, no. How is that problem that you told me about several years ago?"

"Oh, that! No, that's past. I don't even remember it anymore. I don't have any problem with that any more."

God had healed all that pain that she had been unable to forget for so many years.

In order to understand the psychological healing that Jesus gives to us through His cross, we need to understand how our psyche functions. We will look at this in the next chapter.

CHAPTER 2

The Function of the Mind

How it is possible that things that happened in the past can still cause us so much trouble today? We may say, "Oh, no, that doesn't hurt so much now," or "No, I've forgotten that." But we suffer from depression and complexes. Why does this happen? To understand this we must understand how our minds, or psyches, function.

The Conscious

We all know that we have a conscious part of our minds which is aware of what happens around us. We can illustrate the conscious in this way.

<Insert Image 5>

If we are listening to a speaker in a conference room, one part of our conscious focuses on what the speaker is saying. At the same time, with another part of our conscious, we are aware that the lights are turned on, that someone is or isn't sitting by our side, and, if we are close to a highway, of the noises of the traffic passing by. If we focus on a baby crying in the back of the room we become only dimly aware, with another part of our conscious, of what the speaker is saying. But, in one way or another, we are conscious of many things occurring in the room.

The Subconscious

CAN YOU REMEMBER WHAT HAPPENED yesterday at exactly this time? Possibly you were working in the house or in the office, or traveling somewhere. Remembering what happened is quite easy. But can you remember what happened two weeks ago? One month ago? One year ago? Five years ago? Each time it becomes more difficult to remember. This is because, below the conscious level of the mind, we find the subconscious.

We can illustrate in the following way:

<Insert Image 6>

Our daily experiences and impressions are perceived in the conscious part of our minds. It is quite easy to remember things immediately after they happened. But after a while the experience sinks down into the subconscious, and only by concentrating can we remember what happened.

The more time passes, the more difficult it is to remember the incident.

The Unconscious

CAN YOU REMEMBER WHAT YOU DID FIVE, ten, or fifteen years ago? When that memory enters the unconscious, we are unable to recall the incident. We can illustrate it in this way:

<Insert Image 7>

This process is called passive forgetting. It is normal and good. How unbearable it would be to be conscious of everything we have ever experienced! There would be no room in our minds for new experiences.

Another kind of forgetting is called active forgetting. When something happens which is too painful to bear, the mind automatically represses it. Within the unconscious we can imagine a repression line, such as in the following illustration:

<Insert Image 8>

When the mind represses something too painful to bear we cannot remember the incident. But the memory has not died. This can be demonstrated by some kinds of cerebral surgery when the patient is not entirely put to sleep. If small electrodes are placed in his brain and a light electric current passed through them, he may suddenly hear a lullaby from his childhood. When the electrodes are moved, he may recall the face of a long lost friend or hear a conversation in which he had part but had forgotten about.

This means that the things we have experienced are not truly forgotten; we simply cannot recall them back into our conscious mind. Our inability to remember what happened does not mean that the memory has ceased to exist. What happened has been stored down in the unconscious part of our mind. This process of repression can be shown in the illustration on the following page.

When we repress things, we believe we have forgotten what happened, but the memory is still alive. Later we repress other happenings and later still others. Finally, from deep within they begin to project there pain, and we act in ways that we ourselves do not understand.

<Insert Image 9>

We may even try to trigger this process of repression by saying, "I'm going to forget that," or, "Don't talk about that anymore!" We may even ask God to help us to forget what happened. But even if we do manage to "forget it," that does not mean that the memory has died. Why is this so?

Our memories are stored in our unconscious as pictures or scenes of what happened; we could compare them to a movie on a video cassette. Together with the scenes are recorded the emotions we felt at the time when the scenes took place. When we see or experience something that resembles a part of the stored memory, the original emotions are aroused and projected onto what we are experiencing at the moment. We re-experience what we felt at the time of the original experience.

In our unconscious we have no concept of the passage of time or of the usage of words. The concepts of time and words are a part of our conscious and subconscious. Because of this we can talk and talk about what happened, but unless a change occurs in the scenes stored in our memories, the pain will continue. God knows all about this and He has promised to give us something beautiful in exchange for the ashes we carry stored up in our memories. He wants to give a beautiful ending the painful memory.

Without a new ending to the painful memories, any person or any experience can be overshadowed with projected pain, fear, insecurity or any other emotion from an experience that may have happened many years in our past.

Miss Tiffany

WHEN I WAS STUDYING NURSING I HAD five Nursing Arts teachers who taught us how to make beds, give injections, etc. Every time Miss Tiffany supervised my performance I felt as though I had two left hands and ten thumbs. I could never do anything right for her. If one of the other four supervised me, I did very well. I had worked in a hospital as a nurse's aide and knew how to do many of the procedures, so I couldn't understand why everything went wrong when she was around.

One day Miss Tiffany called me aside and asked why I behaved so differently when she supervised me. I was so frightened of her that I could hardly answer her question. In a very soft voice I assured her that nothing at all was wrong, that everything was perfectly all right. I didn't dare tell her that just being close to her frightened me.

Two years later when I studied psychiatric nursing, I realized that Miss Tiffany's facial features were very similar to those of my third grade teacher who had terrified me. Among other things, she made me stand on the platform twice in front of the whole class for something I had not done.

I was so terrified of her that I couldn't talk out loud. My voice would sink into a whisper. Then she would say to me in frustration, "Outside you can play and shout and scream like any normal child. Why can't you talk loud enough in here with me so that I can hear what you're saying?" But the more she scolded, the lower my voice sank. All I could do was sit in terror and wait until she went away.

Now, twelve years later, everything I did for Miss Tiffany turned out wrong, even though she had never done anything to me. When she asked me what was wrong, I found my voice sinking into a tiny whisper. I could only assure her that everything was completely okay–hoping she would go away and leave me alone.

I had forgotten about my third grade teacher. Yet that unrecallable memory made me act in a way that I could not explain. The memory had not died. It was very much alive and active.

Alice and Gloria's stories show in how many layers and how very deeply our experiences and emotions can be repressed.

Alice

ALICE HAD PROBLEMS WITH EVERYONE WITH whom she worked. Not that she herself ever had problems, she told me, it was the other people who always made trouble for her. One day I asked her about her childhood: how had it been, what were the traumas she had suffered.

"Doña Arline," she said emphatically, "I am not like other people who remember all about their past. I don't remember anything of my childhood. I can't remember anything of my life from before I was eleven years old. The only thing I can remember is that they told me that when I was born my brother was so happy he went to all the neighbors and told them he had a new little sister. Other than that I don't remember anything."

I asked myself, "Could it be that this is the root of her problems. Was her childhood so painful that everything has been repressed?"

Sometime later Alice again had an argument, this time with a friend. She wanted to talk with me about the situation, but we were unable to meet for three months. By then she was hardly able to remember what had happened.

"I think this is how it was," she said, "but I just can't remember the details. This always happens to me when I experience something that hurts me. Within a very short time I can't remember the details anymore."

That day we prayed through all the painful things that she could remember. We also asked God to bring back to her memory everything she had "forgotten."

We did not see each other again until a year later. "Guess what?" she said, "I can remember much more of my childhood now."

Originally Alice's repression was almost complete. But when she brought what she could remember to Jesus for healing, other deeper, more painful experiences came to the surface.

Recently Alice once again had problems with someone who didn't understand her. This new pain brought to her memory other traumatic experiences that she had "forgotten." She remembered that she had never been allowed to talk to her parents about anything negative. They could not tolerate problems. Alice always had to show a happy, carefree attitude.

This resulted in her feeling rejected by her parents, and she rejected them in turn. But since she could not tolerate the idea that she had rejected her parents, Alice rejected herself. Later when she accepted Jesus as her Savior, she could not accept this rejection process because she believed a Christian had to be perfect. As a result she repressed the whole process. When Alice finally recognized this complicated process of rejection and gave it to Jesus to carry to the cross, her life began to change.

Gloria

GLORIA LIVED WITH US AS A STUDENT AT the seminary in Colombia, where I was the school nurse and clinical counselor. We did not realize that she looked upon my husband and me as her parents. While we were away on vacation, they called to inform me as the school nurse, that Gloria was very ill. Upon our return we found her completely confused. She wanted to preach to everyone about Jesus. Barefoot and in pajamas, she preached to the boys in their dormitory. She preached to the cats and the dogs. When she could find nothing else, she preached to the furniture and the wind.

Gloria's mother, who had spent some time in mental hospitals, had been most loving to her for the first five years of her life. After that, it seemed she could never please her mother in any way. Everything Gloria did seemed to displeased her mother. She would say to the younger children, "Gloria is a good-for-nothing. You need never pay any attention to what she says."

Every Sunday her mother locked the children into the house and went to church. Gloria was made responsible to see that none of the younger children misbehaved or damaged anything. Of course, no one paid any attention to her and everyone did just what he pleased. When her mother returned, Gloria would be scolded for the children's behavior.

"Look," she would scream, "I said you were a good-for-nothing! Look what those children have done!"

To the children she would repeat, "I told you Gloria was a good-fornothing. You need never pay any attention to what she says."

Eventually Gloria could endure no more and went to live with a married sister. Her sister accepted her and for a time Gloria had a good home. However, three years later her sister and her husband, a pastor, were commissioned to work in a church in a remote part of the jungle. Gloria was unable to accompany them. Since she had no other place to go, she came to the Seminary to study, leaving her boyfriend behind.

It was a very pleasant experience to have Gloria in our home. She was very diligent and helped in every way possible. When the students came for coffee breaks they would all rush off for classes, leaving the dirty dishes behind. Gloria never left until the last cup was washed and returned to its place.

When the semester ended all the students went home for vacation. Since Gloria had nowhere to go, she remained in the seminary and worked in the library. When we left for vacation, Gloria went to visit her boyfriend. In his church she found a new girl who told her, "I am madly in love with your boyfriend. I'm going to have a witch cast a spell on him that will make him leave you and come to me."

Poor Gloria! She felt that her mother had abandoned her, her sister had abandoned her by moving and we had abandoned her by going on vacation. The only one she had left was her boyfriend. Now she was going to lose him too. She could take no more. She became mentally ill.

I flew with her to another city to a Christian psychiatrist who agreed to treat her in his home. When he asked who her father and mother were, Gloria responded, "Don Carlos and Doña Arline" (my husband and I). She could no longer recall who her parents were. They had caused her so much pain that her mind had repressed all knowledge of them. She needed several weeks of treatment before she could remember that we were not her parents.

All this shows how our painful memories can be repressed to such a degree that we think they are gone. But they are not dead; we are simply unable to recall them.

When I was doing graduate studies, one of my classes required a practice period in a day care clinic. What drew my attention during this time was the fact that we helped these people verbalize and relive their trauma and then in essence had to tell them, "Now accept that this is what happened and live with it."

These people did get better; their experiences did hurt less. They could live with them more easily. With psychology we can help a person look at his past difficulties, traumas and problems, and live with them in such a way that they hurt less. But we cannot remove them. There is no psychology on earth that can re-do the past. Only Jesus can enter into our past and carry its pain. This does not mean that He changes the past or makes us forget what happened.

Many people seem to believe that if our memories were healed, our past would be changed in some way, or that we can no longer remember what happened. However, if we are unable to remember what happened, it means the incident has been repressed. If we are healed, we can remember what happened, but it doesn't hurt anymore. This psychological healing is similar to our physical healing as the following illustration shows.

The Scar

I HAVE A TWO-INCH SCAR ON MY RIGHT knee. I remember clearly what caused it. When I was about eight years old I propped a tire on my knees while my brother cut through it with a big butcher knife. Suddenly the knife slipped through the tire and into my knee. I remember very well how the blood spurted and how I screamed.

If the wound were not healed, I would keep it bandaged. I would watch closely that no one would come too close or try to look at it or even talk about it. If anyone would try to remove the bandage I would become very defensive because of the pain it would cause me.

On the other hand, I might go about with my wound uncovered, pointing it out and saying, "Do you see what my brother did to me? That's the kind of brother I have. You can't imagine how he made me suffer!" I would act in one extreme or the other. As it is, I need to do neither of these because my knee is healed. The scar is there. I can remember exactly what happened, but I feel no pain.

This is what happens with our painful memories when they have been healed. We do not need to hide the hurts of our past. Neither do we constantly need to talk about them. They have been healed and the pain they had caused is gone.

Children suffer psychologically when their basic needs are not met. In the next chapter we will look at some basic human needs that must be met in childhood, if the person is to function freely as an adult.

CHAPTER 3

Basic Human Needs

EVERY HUMAN BEING HAS BASIC needs which must be filled during childhood. If these needs are not adequately filled, the person will have difficulties functioning freely as an adult.

We have primary basic needs such as food, water, shelter and air. If these needs were not met, we would die. We also have secondary basic needs which are so important that unless children have them met in a way they can feel and accept, they will suffer psychologically later on in life. The following examples show us some of these basic needs.

Love

BABIES CAN DIE FROM LACK OF LOVE AND attention. Yet a newborn is like an empty receptacle who cannot give back love. The newborn cannot think, "I love my mother so much that I will not cry at 2:00 in the morning when I'm hungry. I will wait until she gets awake by herself."

No newborn can produce that kind of love. A baby will cry, no matter how inconvenient the timing is for the parents.

The parents must pour love, and more love, into the baby's "empty receptacle" until it is full and begins to overflow. The love must be expressed in ways such that the baby and child can feel loved. When this emotional receptacle is filled and overflows, the child is able to give love. The receptacle must constantly be replenished with love if it is to continue overflowing.

If this receptacle is never filled, the child, and later the adult, will not be able to give love freely. Worse yet, the receptacle will become like a bottomless pit which no amount of love will be able to fill. Such children never really feel loved. There is never a sense of being filled and satiated. Later as an adult, they may marry a spouse who gives them endless love, but in spite of this they will not feel loved. Neither can they give love freely without calculating what they will receive in return. They do not feel loved by God.

If at the age of five years something interrupts the flow of love, we could say that the receptacle has a bottom, but it has sprung a leak at the five year level. Some emotional part of this child will not be able to develop beyond the five year level. This person as an adult will feel that there is still a fiveyear-old child somewhere inside of himself.

How can such a small baby know whether he or she is loved? The baby cannot even understand what is meant when the parents say, "I love you."

In a penal institution several psychologists studied mothers who were about to give birth. They wanted to know whether they could tell by their actions which mothers would keep their babies and which ones would give them up for adoption. The mothers themselves had not decided what they would do. Very soon the psychologists could predict what their decisions would be. How could they tell?

When the mothers who kept their babies received their newborn into their arms, they first touched the baby's head with the tips of their fingers, then stroked him gently with the palms of their hands. Later they checked his arms, his abdomen and legs. They counted the toes and fingers, then wrapped the baby back into the blanket and gave him the bottle. The mothers who did not keep their babies received them into their arms and immediately stuck the bottle into their mouths.

If these psychologists could predict which mothers would keep their babies, how much more must a baby feel the difference in the way it is handled when the mother doesn't really love and want him or her. Later the child/adult will feel a deep inner sense of rejection that nothing seems to be able to touch.

Jesse

IN OUR OWN FAMILY WE HAD THE SAD experience of a child who did not feel loved. One of our relatives did not live the Christian life he professed. When his girlfriend became pregnant they were quickly married so that no one would become aware of what had happened. After their marriage, they realized that they had very little in common.

As parents they soon tired of the fact that one of them had to remain at home with Jesse. Eventually they decided that once a week they would put him in his crib and go to their separate places of entertainment. Almost three years later the marriage ended in divorce. Jesse was sent to live with a great-aunt who really loved and cared for him. However, she was nearly seventy years old and could not keep him for more than one year.

When one of Jesse's uncles married, he and his wife offered to give him a home. Jesse sensed what was going to happen and begged his aunt to keep him. "Auntie," he would beg, "I can stay with you, can't I? You won't send me away, will you?" But the day came when he had to go with his uncle.

Jesse's uncle and aunt loved him. They assured him that this was his new family; he would stay with them forever because they were his new daddy and mamma. When he asked why his own mother didn't love and want him, they carefully explained that his real mommy did love him, but her love was more like an aunt's love. Eventually Jesse came to accept his new family and the two brothers and a sister that soon arrived.

One day his mother took him home with her for a month of vacation. During that time she assured Jesse that she really did love him; that he was her son and she loved him like all good mothers, and that his new mother actually only loved him like an aunt. When the month passed she took him back to live with his aunt.

By now poor Jesse was totally confused. If his mother loved him like a mother and his aunt like an aunt, why did his mother make him live with his aunt who said that she loved him like a mother and that his mother loved him like an aunt? The only thing Jesse could do was sit on his bed and listen to a record his mother had given him when she left. He couldn't play, or go to kindergarten.

Finally, his new mother (his aunt) took him to a psychologist. He had to attend a school for disturbed children. Jesse became a stooped, walking skeleton with his shoulders bent and drawn together. He suffered from asthma. His new mother and father showered Jesse with love, but he was unable to feel loved. The psychologist told them this did not begin with the divorce; it had begun in his early infancy when he was left alone in his crib for hours and hours.

One day Jesse's real mother decided to take him home and care for him herself. She tried to be a good mother. She took him to a psychologist and enrolled him in a good school. However, when her vacation time came she didn't want to take Jesse with her. Instead, she left him with his father and stepmother and traveled abroad with her lover.

Over the years Jesse's asthma had become worse and worse. His mother had decided that on her return from her vacation, he would spend two weeks on an island at a special retreat for asthmatic children. Since he was a big boy now, he would travel there all by himself by train. Jesse, however, hated to sleep in any bed other than his own. He hated the whole idea.

Several days before his mother's return, Jesse suffered an asthma attack and had to be hospitalized. His mother returned on a Wednesday and immediately signed him out of the hospital so that he would be ready to leave for the island on Friday. On their way home, he had another asthma attack. She rushed him back to the hospital, but he died on the way. Jesse was buried on his tenth birthday.

I asked a psychiatrist friend whether the final cause of this child's death could have been the result of his unmet need for love. He answered that that was surely the underlying cause of it all. In spite of the fact that Jesse received so much love later on, his "receptacle" had become a bottomless pit. He simply could not feel loved.

Jesse's life is a drastic example. But how many people walk around with "bottomless pits" inside themselves.

They cannot feel love and appreciation because they did not receive enough love expressed in a way they could understand, when they were small.

One day when we were living in northern Colombia, I went to a laundry to pick up some clothes. The laundry was operated from a room in the owner's house. Inside I could hear a child, possibly two years old, screaming and crying in anguish and terror. Since I needed my husband's clothes I waited, thinking that someone would come to care for the child. I waited for twenty minutes. In all that time the child did not stop screaming and crying. Since it was Monday morning I could not tell if the parents were so drunk that they could not hear the child, or if they had actually locked him or her inside alone.

How many children are left in these conditions! They cry and cry and no one cares for them; or if care is provided, it is done with displeasure or even with abuse.

A friend of mine was in the hospital for the birth of her fifth child. In the same room was a woman whose husband did not believe in birth control. Their thirteenth child had just been born; their oldest one was sixteen years old. She received her new daughter into her arms in tears. In her exhausted state, it would be nearly impossible for this mother to give her child all the love and attention it would need.

A child may not receive enough love because his mother died, or his parents divorced and his stepmother does not care for him. Perhaps she was left in a hospital for a long time and was separated from her parents. Perhaps family problems and arguments prevented the parents from expressing their love. Maybe the parents themselves had not received enough love and were unable to give love in a way that he could understand. Perhaps the father was an alcoholic and mistreated the family or caused them such shame that the mother could not function in her role as a mother. Maybe the child was born during a time of violence or war when there was so much fear that there was no time for love.

Pardon

ANOTHER BASIC NEED EVERY CHILD HAS is to receive pardon. If a child is not forgiven for his errors he will not be able to forgive others as an adult. As Christians we say that we must forgive those who have wronged us. So the person kneads his emotions, trying to produce some kind of feeling that resembles forgiveness. He says he forgives the one who has done him wrong, and then represses the pain that the incident caused him.

We cannot give more forgiveness than we have received. Many people have been so deeply hurt that they simply cannot forgive the one who has injured them. In spite of this, since they know that Christians must forgive, they try and try to produce feelings of forgiveness, and feel most guilty if unable to do so. Many of us are destitute of the capacity to forgive. We do not have it and cannot produce it. Parents must pour pardon into the child's emotional receptacle until it overflows lest he become a "bottomless pit" and can never truly forgive.

Ana Cecilia

ANA CECILIA WAS BORN INTO A VERY dysfunctional family. Her father was a gambler. He lost large sums of money. Ana Cecilia followed his example. When she was five years old she gambled away five pesos her mother had given her to run an errand.

When her father heard what she had done, he tied her writs together, hooked them across a spike in a rafter of the palm-thatched roof of their house and beat her with a belt until he was too tired to continue. Then the mother continued the beating until she was exhausted. When the little girl fainted, they plunged her into a tank of cold water to revive her, only to hang her up again and continue the beating. For the following week, she was shut into the bedroom naked to show her what a bad girl she had been.

The little girl's life went from bad to worse. At the age of seven she was repeatedly raped by her brother. Later she had three children by her uncle and after that two others by two other men. Besides all this, the insatiable desire to gamble continually plagued her.

One day she heard the gospel and gave her life to Jesus. But she had no real peace. She had great difficulty to forgive those with whom she worked. The smallest error would bring a strong reprimand from her. Ana Cecilia told me, "I always think, 'If I could be strung up for five pesos, why can't these people be held accountable for what they did?'"

We had a special time together to pray through her cruel punishment. I insisted that she express out loud exactly how she felt about her father's treatment.

"He is unjust," she said. "What he did was unjust."

"Then say to the memory of your father, 'Father, you are unjust'."

Ana Cecilia remained quiet for some time. Finally she said, "It isn't true that my father is unjust."

"What is he then?" I asked.

"He is . . . he is . . . he is a demon!" she screamed. "He is a demon!"

"Say then to the father in your memory, 'Father, you are a demon. I can never forgive what you have done to me!'"

Ana Cecilia broke into tears. "Yes, that is the truth. I can never forgive you, Father. You are a demon!"

I put my hand gently on Ana Cecilia's shoulder to console her. "Tell the whole truth to Jesus. Say, 'Jesus, I hate my father. I wish he would die. I never want to see him again!'"

"Yes, Jesus, that is the truth," she sobbed. "I hate him! I hate him! I want him to die! I never want to see him again!"

"Now tell Jesus," I gently urged, "'Jesus, I can no longer bear this hatred. Inside myself, it's killing me. Jesus, I give to you the hatred, the injustice, the humiliation that I felt. I cast it all on you. Carry it for me. I cannot carry this any longer.'"

Ana Cecilia followed the prayer with her whole heart and continued, sobbing: "Jesus, I cannot forgive my father. I pour this pain onto you. I can't carry it. Fill me with your forgiveness.

"Father, although I have nothing in me that can forgive what you have done to me, I open myself to receive the forgiveness that Jesus is pouring into me. I take Jesus' forgiveness and give it to you. Father, with Jesus' forgiveness I forgive you. I set you free from what you did to me. By God's grace and power, I will no longer hold this against you. Forgive me, too, when I did not act right towards you."

In this same way Ana Cecilia also forgave her mother. Only in this way could she be freed from the desire to revenge her past on others. Her pain had been so great that she could never have produced feelings of forgiveness.

If someone has wronged you so terribly that you cannot forgive him, tell the truth. Jesus says in John 6:32, "The truth will make you free."

Protection

A THIRD BASIC NEED OF EVERY CHILD IS protection. Every child needs to feel secure. He needs to feel that his parents function like a protecting wall between him and the danger-filled world around him. Often this protective wall is missing. Sometimes the very parents who should be protecting the child will themselves plant fears into him with such exclamations as, "Watch out! The policeman will get you!" or "If you aren't good the bogey man will carry you away tonight!"

Even though the parents may try to protect the child, circumstances may be such that the child cannot be protected. Felipe (Hans) was one of these children.

Felipe

I WILL NEVER FORGET FELIPE, WHO WAS preparing for the ministry. He came to see me because he felt he spoke too harshly to others. He didn't want to speak that way, but he always did.

Felipe (Hans) was born at the very beginning of World War II. His father was deeply involved in politics and worked against the Nazis. Finally his father had to flee. For a long time no one knew if he was dead or alive.

One day Hans' mother told the children they were all going on a picnic. Suddenly Hans found himself on an airplane alone with his younger sister. None of them knew where they were going. They both cried and cried. When

Hans saw his sister nearly crazed with fear, he stopped his own crying in order to calm her.

When the plane landed in Switzerland, strangers met them and took them to a boarding school. They had to learn a new language and culture. After one year their parents suddenly appeared and took them to Spain to live. There they attended a new school with another language.

In Spain the whole family lived together until their father had to leave again. Then the mother and children returned to their native country via Germany by train. From the train Hans saw houses on fire and people fleeing in panic. The dead were lying everywhere. They had no assurance that they would arrive at their destination. Soon after arriving home, they again had to flee to Spain. When the war ended, their father came to them in Spain.

One day the father said to his son, "Hans, we are going to the United States. From now on you must use your real name. You aren't Hans. That is just a name we called you in order to hide you. You are actually Felipe."

Upon arriving in the United States, Felipe found himself in another school with yet another language and culture. He tried hard to behave like an American, but despite all his efforts his grades dropped. Everything began going wrong even though Felipe was very intelligent. Perhaps his high intelligence made him even more sensitive to his difficulties.

Eventually he was put into a special school, where he slowly started to recuperate. Later he was admitted to a specialized university because of his great intelligence. Again he could not cope, and had to leave.

Felipe's life continued downward until one day he found Jesus as his Savior. He found forgiveness for his sins and began living a new life. Now he was preparing for the ministry. However, Felipe found himself dealing harshly and abruptly with his parishioners. If they didn't do everything perfectly to his liking, he tongue-lashed them. He couldn't understand why he behaved in this way.

After Felipe recounted his story, I told him he would need to open up and relive his past pain in order to give it to Jesus to carry for him. For several weeks he was unable to feel anything. One day we prayed that God himself would open the door to the past where everything was repressed.

Felipe returned the next week with a smile on his face. When he had been praying he saw with his "spiritual eyes" that God gave him a set of keys.

"I saw something like a dungeon with a heavy door," Felipe said. "I took a key and opened the door. Inside I saw a little boy crying. I felt that child was me. I spoke to him in my mother tongue. I told him, 'Jesus has taken care of all your problems. You can come out now.' The little boy came out of the dungeon.

"Beside me was another heavy door. I tried to unlock it with another key. The door opened. Inside I saw another boy, a little bigger. I spoke to him in German since I was sure that the child in there in the darkness and loneliness was myself. I told him everything was all right. The boy came out.

"I opened another door and found another child a bit bigger, crying and trembling with fear. I told him in Spanish, 'You can come out now. Jesus has taken care of everything.' This boy also came out.

"Then I opened the last door. There was a teenager to whom I spoke in English, telling him that he could come out.

"You know," Felipe told me, "I feel so much better, but I'm scared.

Those dungeons are still there. Suppose I would get back into them again!"

"Let's pray again," I told him. "Let's ask Jesus to carry those dungeons to the cross."

I asked God to open Felipe's spiritual eyes so that he could "see" how Jesus carried everything for him.

After we prayed Felipe said, "I 'saw' all those dungeons turn into cardboard, roll up and disappear into the sea. Now I see in the place where they had been a very beautiful landscape beside the sea, filled with little red brick houses, like a landscape in Spain. Do you know something? My fear is gone!"

Jesus had taken on himself everything that had happened. After that Felipe began to notice a change in the way he treated others.

Praise

ANOTHER BASIC NEED OF EACH CHILD is to be praised. The newborn doesn't know anything about himself–not even that he exists. He does not know where his body ends and the crib begins. There he lies, beautiful, lovable; but he knows nothing about himself, although he has great potential.

It was very interesting to watch our children when they were several months old. They would stick their toes into their mouths and bite them hard and then cry as though someone had done something awful to them. They did not know that those wiggly, pink toes were part of their body.

Since the newborn knows nothing about himself, he does not know whether he is a person of worth or someone completely worthless. Yet by the time he becomes an adult he will have formed a concept of who he is, what he can do and what he is worth. The only way he will know what kind of person he is, is from what those around him say about him; first the parents and siblings and, later, others outside the family.

If the child is frequently told that he can't do anything right, is stupid, dumb or inferior, sooner or later he will come to believe that he is an untalented person of very little worth. Too often a child is told, "You are so stupid!"

While living on the north coast of Colombia we visited many homes in our church planting ministries. Often parents would present their children to us, saying something like, "This is Blanca. She has really turned out well. But this is Negrita. She isn't worth anything!"

This, of course, made Negrita feel she was totally worthless; and this is what she will come to believe about herself. Blanca, on the other hand, will know that she is not nearly as perfect as her parents said she was. Deep within herself she will know that she also acts stupidly at times. She will know that she can never measure up to her parents' expectations and will also feel worthless.

Elvia

ELVIA WAS A PSYCHOLOGIST WHO HAD recently given her life to the Lord in a church in Colombia.

As was the custom, she was asked to give a testimony of what Jesus had done in her life. Elvia always answered, "But what am I going to say in a testimony? I was happy before and now I'm still happy. It's not worth saying that."

This continued for such a long time that I finally concluded something was not right in her life. A month later we received a call from a young believer at 10:30 p.m., asking us to come to Elvia's house where several people had been praying for her friend for two days for deliverance from demon oppression. We went to see what we could do to help. There we learned that the two girls had been living in a lesbian relationship.

The following day they called again because they had been awake all night. We finally brought Elvia to our home since she was too scared to settle down. I gave her some medication to quiet her and stayed by her bedside until she fell asleep. The following morning she seemed completely calm and left the city.

After about three months Elvia returned to tell me that she intended to return to her old life again. Her new life just wasn't worth living.

After talking at great length with her, I had to give up and said, "Fine, then, go back. I can't keep you from going. God Himself won't keep you if you want to go. You can go, but be sure of one thing: God says, 'Today, if you hear his voice, harden not your heart.' If you go back, don't expect that it will be easy to get out the second time."

"But, this life just isn't worth the trouble," she cried. "And what's more, you can't help me because you are a woman. This thing that is inside of me tells me only a man can help me."

Elvia almost had me convinced until the Holy Spirit showed me the lie. "That is a lie," I told her. "Before God, men and women have access to the same power. Furthermore, I am not going to cast out that thing. It's Jesus, the perfect Man, who will cast it out."

At that precise moment, one of the other women professors came to our apartment. Together we cast out demons of fear, lesbianism, hate, anger and many more.

Then Elvia told me the story of her life. She did not really know who was her mother. She did not know if she belonged to her aunt, who always understood her but was unmarried and had given her to the one she called mother, or if she belonged to the one she called mother, but who hated her and therefore gave her to her aunt to care for much of the time. Every time she tried to talk to her mother about this, she would only laugh and refuse to answer.

"I know that my mother didn't love me," Elvia continued. "She always said, 'The color of your skin is just like your grandmother's, and I hate her. You're just a good-for-nothing. You are so stupid you will never be good for anything.'"

Elvia's parents were able to send her to one of the best private schools in the city. At the same time they told her she was so stupid she would never be able to learn anything. But her grades were very good. In the third year her grades were outstanding.

The little girl grabbed her report card and ran home thinking, "Now my mother will finally see that I am not as stupid as she thought."

Her mother was sitting in the living room when the little girl arrived. She ran to her side and shouted, "Mama, look at my grades! Look! I'm not stupid!"

Her mother took the report card in her hand, looked at it, then sniffed, "Hmm! These aren't your grades. You are entirely too stupid to get grades like this! You are your teacher's pet; that's why she gave you the grades. You will never be able to get grades like this!"

Elvia finished high school and entered the university to study psychology, graduating near the top of her class. It was during her time in the university that her relationship with her girlfriend began.

After graduating Elvia worked as a psychologist in a school. One day she was sent an eleven year old girl who had begun an unhealthy relationship with another girl. Elvia asked, "What could I tell her? I had the same problem. The only thing I could tell her was that she had to accept herself as she was. Since I had no answer for myself, how could I give her one?"

Elvia and I prayed through her life. When we came to the part where she ran into the living room with her report card, I prayed that God would open her spiritual eyes so that she could see Jesus in their living room.

"Elvia," I asked, "with your spiritual eyes can you imagine Jesus sitting in your living room?"

"Yes, I see Him in the big chair," she answered.

"Take your report card and, instead of running to your mother, run to Jesus. Show Him your grades and see what He says about them."

Suddenly Elvia began to cry and sob. When she quieted down she exclaimed, "Jesus was sitting there and I took my report card and ran to Him. He took me on his lap, snuggled me into his arms and said, 'I believe that these are your grades, and that you earned them. You are my daughter and I am very proud of you.'"

At that moment Jesus took on himself the terrible pain that Elvia had been carrying for so long. We prayed through the rest of her life, but I felt that at that instant something very special had happened in her. God had healed the root of Elvia's problem. She had desperately looked for a mother. This had been the underlying motive that had brought about her unhealthy relationship.

When I last heard from Elvia, she was working with university students, bringing to them the healing she found in Jesus. When asked to give a testimony, she did not hesitate. She knew what God has done in her life.

All of these are examples of people whose basic needs were not met in their childhood. Such a child will suffer from deep feelings of insecurity and inferiority as an adult. In the next chapter we will look at these emotions.

CHAPTER 4

Feelings of Inferiority

ALL OF US HAVE FEELINGS OF inferiority. All of us have been born into a race of fallen human beings. There are no perfect parents or homes. The simple fact that we are members of a fallen human race, living in a fallen world, already tells us that we will not always have all our basic needs filled in a way that we can understand and feel.

Every child will feel misunderstood, hurt and rejected at times. If the parents find, understand and bring healing to these traumas, the child will grow up without major psychological problems. But sometimes children cannot explain what has happened to them. Or, as we mentioned in the last chapter, sometimes parents are so traumatized themselves that they simply cannot give the child what he or she needs. Although the parents try to meet their children's needs, their circumstances may be such that the child's needs cannot always be met.

Many people have acute feelings of inferiority. We can illustrate these feelings with a thermometer or scale as in the following illustration.

<Insert Image 10>

Jesus was the only person who did not have feelings of inferiority. He felt neither inferior nor superior. We could say that He was at the zero point on the thermometer.

In John 13 we read that Jesus knew where He had come from and where He was going. He knew who He was. He was God, but He did not feel superior. He was nailed to a cross, but did not feel inferior. He could confront kings, but did not feel too superior to talk with the Samaritan woman drawing water from a well. Because He knew who He was, He could lay aside his garments, stoop down and wash his disciples' feet.

None of us will ever achieve the equilibrium of Jesus until we see Him face to face. We will always find ourselves somewhere below the zero point. Unlike Jesus, none of us really knows where we have come from, who we are, or where we're going.

According to the degree of our feelings of inferiority, we must find something that makes us feel superior in order to fill the deficiency. We cannot live in a continual deficit; it would finally lead us to suicide. Our feelings of superiority become mechanisms we use to defend ourselves from feeling inadequate. If we feel inferior to a fourth degree, we will need to find something to make us feel superior to a fourth degree in order to make our lives endurable.

How do we behave when we feel inferior? The following stories show some defense mechanisms and give us clues to our behavior.

Isolation

Norma was a student at the seminary. She could never be friends with any of the other students. She always kept to herself. When asked about this Norma replied, "The problem is, they always get me into trouble."

According to Norma, she herself never had problems. All her problems and difficulties originated in those around her. It became clear that she felt very inferior; we could say to a third degree. She filled this deficiency with three degrees of superiority of "never having any problems." Anything that interfered with "not having any problems" had to be rejected. Therefore, Norma withdrew from the others around her. Being without problems gave her a sense of self-worth.

Drawing Attention

We often try to be the center of attention. While everyone pays attention to us we feel we must be worth something.

Pablo repeatedly reminded me, "I am a professional person. You are a professional person just like I am a professional person."

Pablo suffered from severe feelings of inferiority. Through making great sacrifices, he had finally been able to graduate from college. As a professional person, he had some sense of self-worth. He filled his deep feelings of inferiority with his profession.

Hypersensitivity

The person who feels inferior becomes overly sensitive. He feels everyone around him is superior. When he is criticized, he feels pushed down another degree. This causes an even greater deficit, which the person may not have the inner resources to fill. He must therefore reject the criticism that caused the deficit.

The other extreme may also appear. Pablo, the professional person, rejected all praise. One day I commended him for a talk he had given in the seminary. He answered me abruptly, "Don't tell me that. I'm not a friend of people who praise me! I want people to tell me what I do wrong!"

Pablo responded in this way because he feared he had defects. To him, the fact that he wanted to hear about his defects meant that he was mature enough to confront his errors and was therefore a person of real worth. To receive praise made him feel immature and unaware of what he feared people saw in him. He filled his feelings of inferiority with an eagerness to hear about his defects.

Unlike a person with feelings of inferiority, which make him continually seek or reject praise, Jesus received both praise and criticism without feeling either superior or inferior.

Possessiveness

People who feel inferior can become very possessive. They may be heard saying such things as, "Those are my things. Don't you touch them!"

Several of the teenage girls in one of the churches we pastored felt inferior and insecure. They constantly vied with each other to be the best friend with those whom they considered to be in the "in" group. If someone else became too friendly with their best friend, that became a reason to stop coming to church. They were often heard saying, "She took away my best friend. I'm not coming back anymore."

These girls filled their feelings of inferiority by identifying with the popularity of their friends. The more popular their best friend, the greater their feelings of self-worth. The greater the inferiority complex, the more popular the best friend needed to be, and the more fragile the friendship. Their self-worth quickly disappeared when they believed they had lost this person's undivided friendship.

Perfectionism

SOME PEOPLE TRY TO DO EVERYTHING PERFECTLY. If their efforts result in something with a flaw, they feel worthless. If their feelings of inferiority is only at the first degree, they have room to be quite flexible. But if they feel inferior to a fifth degree on our scale, they must fill it with five degrees of perfectionism. If Gloria, the girl who thought we were her parents (Chapter 1), visited us for coffee break and left before every cup was back in place, she felt worthless. Her sense of self-worth came from doing everything perfectly right.

Criticism

PEOPLE WHO FEEL INFERIOR OFTEN CRITICIZE others severely. They may say such things as, "He doesn't know anything. He doesn't do anything right. How can he be so stupid?" If a person who feels inferior is able to see the faults of others, he feels there must still be something good about himself. He must not be as bad as those whose faults he can still recognize.

The person who feels inferior is also overly sensitive to criticism. If she passes by several people speaking in a low voice, she will think immediately, "What are they saying about me?" It would never occur to her to think that they could be planning a surprise party for her. She knows that they are saying something bad about her.

Projection

WE SEE IN OTHERS WHAT WE FEAR MAY be found in ourselves. When we say, "See how proud she is!" we may fear our own pride.

In one of my psychology classes, I asked the students to write a short paper about what they disliked about themselves. All the students except Pedro did what I assigned.

Pedro wrote, "What bothers me most is that I find no spiritual people anywhere. The pastor of my church is not spiritual. No one in my church is spiritual. I thought that here in the seminary the professors would be spiritual. I thought the students preparing for the ministry would be spiritual. How surprised I was not to find one spiritual person here. Neither the professors nor the students are spiritual. There is not one spiritual person in this whole seminary."

I called Pedro to my office and asked whether he felt he wasn't very spiritual. He dropped his head and murmured, "Yes."

Pedro was born into a Christian home. As a child, he accepted Jesus as his Savior. When he was eight he had to sleep in the same bed with Alicia, one of his cousins. Although he did not do anything to her, he had entertained thoughts of touching her sexually. Even though he had asked God to forgive him over and over, from that time on Pedro believed he was no good. He was sure that no really spiritual person could ever have had such thoughts.

We prayed together and cast those thoughts on Jesus to carry to the cross. Then Pedro forgave himself for what he had thought. In a short time he saw everyone around him, professors, students and even himself, as being more spiritual.

Compensation

THE PERSON WHO FEELS INFERIOR MUST compensate for his insufficiency in one way or another. Since our apartment was on the campus, it was interesting to observe the freshmen when they came to the seminary. They were outside of their own world. This world was new and unknown. All the walls of protection they had built around themselves in their home communities were lacking. They felt naked and exposed. They didn't know how to act.

One student who was very short began walking with a very heavy step, almost stomping his feet. His footsteps sounded like those of a big, strong man. He teased our little dog and crept up behind the girls to scare them and make them scream.

One day I asked him, "Why do you tease the little animals and the girls? Why don't you tease the big watch dog or the fellows your own size or bigger? Does it make you feel like a strong man when the girls scream?"

"Oh, no," he said. "It's not that. I just like to hear them squeal."

This student felt very inferior for many reasons. He was compensating for his small stature by teasing the small animals and the girls. When we compensate for our feelings of inferiority we never confront people who we see as being on our own level or higher. They would make us lose and we would feel even more worthless.

Your Feelings of Self-Worth

On what do you base your feelings of self-worth? On being a perfectionist? On seeing that those around are worse than you? There is only one source from which true feelings of self-worth should come. You are a person of great worth because you have been made in the image of God. He is the great I AM. It is out of his I AM—His being—that God acts.

We are to reflect God's image. Yet we try to find our identity and selfworth in what we do rather than in what we are. We reverse God's order of being and action. If our self-worth no longer comes from what we do but from who we are in Him, then we can be free from our feelings of inferiority because our worth is no longer based on our performance but on who God is and who we are in Him.

The only way to be freed from feelings of inferiority is to admit the truth. Jesus said "The truth will make you free" (John 8:32). If you admit the truth about what you feel that you are, or are afraid that you are, and about what you have done, Jesus will carry all that to the cross and you will be free. You will have nothing left to hide.

You need not pretend that everything is fine if you feel something is wrong. Perhaps you feel your mother or father did not love you. Or perhaps they were not able to express their love in a way that you could feel. To admit this is not blaming them. It is simply admitting how you feel. After all, our parents are the victims of the traumas suffered in their homes, and their parents were victims of the traumas suffered in their homes, and so on back through the generations.

If you do not admit the truth and receive healing, you will cause hurts in your own children. You do not mean to traumatize them; you simply can't act differently. We cannot act differently from what we are.

Now take a piece of paper and make a list of everything in your life that hurt you. What was your father like? How did your mother treat you? What did they tell you? Don't write what you believe your parents or others thought about the incident. Write what you felt. What did your brothers and sisters tell you about yourself? What did your teachers say?

How did you feel when they told you were no good, a good-for-nothing?

Or possibly they held you up too highly, never acknowledging that you made mistakes, although in your heart you knew you were not as good as they said you were. How did you feel when you were compared with others, possibly with your brother or sister, or when you were punished unjustly and had to keep quiet? Be sincere with God and with yourself as you make out your list. It is the truth that will make you free.

If our basic needs have not been met in an adequate way, there are usually certain areas within us that need healing. We will look at some of these areas in the next chapter.

CHAPTER 5

Healing our Identity

WHO ARE YOU? HAVE YOU accepted yourself, or are you angry with yourself? Do you reject yourself? One girl said, "But how can I love myself with such skinny legs and crooked toes?"

Every person has something about himself that he doesn't like. I remember very well the day I had to accept my freckles. I thought they were most ugly. I wanted darker skin. And there was what I called my mousecolored hair. I thought it was so ugly. I clearly remember the day I accepted the fact that God made me as I am and that to Him I am beautiful.

Have you accepted yourself just as God made you? Or do you hate yourself? What do you reject about yourself? Is your nose too long, your legs too skinny, or your toes too crooked? What makes you reject yourself? Self-rejection has long lasting effects. It can be carried into your marriage and spoil your relationship. Fabio and Flor's story shows how easily selfrejection could have spoiled their marriage.

Fabio

Fabio was the son of a medical doctor who was an alcoholic. Almost every night his father came home drunk. Fabio's earliest memory was of being awakened in the middle of the night by his mother, who frantically pushed him and his four brothers and sisters under their bed because his father was coming home. He could hear his mother scream as his father beat her with his belt, and then felt the bed bounce above him as the belt hit the mattress where he had been sleeping moments before.

Several years before his death, Fabio's father changed and led a more sober life, and his family experienced peace in their home. But Fabio's brothers' and sisters' marriages all ended in fights and separations, just like the marriages of all his aunts and uncles in previous generations. His parents' marriage was the only one that had not ended in separation.

We learned to know Fabio through our friend Flor, a beautiful young lady who had been his exclusive girlfriend for over five years.

We encouraged Fabio and Flor to get married since in Colombia no one would believe that a steady relationship of over five years could not include a sexual relationship. But they weren't interested in marriage. A few weeks later they came to talk to us about the matter.

"I love Flor too much to marry her!" declared Fabio, sitting dejectedly on the sofa in our living room. "I know that if we get married our marriage will break up. Our friendship is so beautiful that I don't want anything to damage it. I can't marry her."

Then Fabio told us the story of his father, and the relationships in all the marriages in his family for several generations.

Together with Fabio, we prayed the painful memories of his life. We asked Jesus to enter into his memory of the bedroom where his father had beaten his mother and to carry the whole scene to the cross. We asked Jesus to heal his eyes, ears and memory that had seen, heard and stored these terrible experiences. We bound and cast out the evils of misunderstanding and separation that had passed from generation to generation. After this Fabio and Flor made plans to get married.

Flor

Two weeks before their wedding, Flor called me for an emergency appointment. "I can't get married," she sobbed later in my office. "I don't know what to do. I am so jealous. If Fabio comes home only five minutes late all I can think of is, `What is he doing now? Which girl is he out with? Who is he talking to? Where did they go?'

"I have fasted over this. I have prayed. But nothing changes. Everything continues the same. I simply can't get married like this!"

I was astonished, because I had known Flor for a long time and believed she was ready to marry. I could only ask God to give me the key that would unlock her problem.

While Flor was telling me her story something drew my attention. "Flor," I asked, "could it be possible that as a child you were compared negatively with others?"

Flor dropped her head and began to cry again, nodding in assent. Flor had two older sisters who, while walking down the streets with her, would say, "Look at that woman. Do you see her nose? That's how your nose looks. Do you see how funny that woman walks? That's how you walk. That's how ugly you are."

Her sisters told Flor that when the neighbors came to see her when she was born, they hid her in another room because they were ashamed to let them see how ugly their new sister was. "You are the ugliest person we have ever seen," they told her over and over. Actually, Flor was a very beautiful young lady, but she did not feel that way.

"Could it be," I asked her, "that you always believed you were so ugly that no man would ever truly be interested in you? Did you feel that even if someone would seem to love you, any other girl would be able to win him away whenever she desired?"

Again Flor's head dropped and fresh tears fell. "Yes, that is exactly how I feel," she sobbed.

I asked Flor to recall all the times someone had told her that she was ugly or undesirable. Together we asked Jesus to walk with her through her life.

"Remember the woman with the ugly nose," I urged her. "Now imagine Jesus walking between you, your sisters and that woman. Tell Jesus exactly what your sisters told you. See how He takes that whole scene on Himself. See how He filters the words and takes out the pain before they come to you. Show Him the woman whose way of walking was so ugly and the ugly baby hidden in the other room. Cast them all on Jesus to carry to the cross."

We asked Jesus to come into every scene. I laid my hands gently over her eyes and ears and asked God to heal them and her emotions that had been so traumatized.

Two weeks later Fabio and Flor were married. A year later, Flor invited me to speak to a group of women she was discipling. I asked permission to use their story in the seminar. After the meeting Flor told me that even though they had been married for over a year they had yet to have their first argument.

Several years later, Flor and Fabio were the parents of two beautiful children. They lived in an apartment close to us, and had one of the most harmonious marriages we have ever known. But imagine how long their marriage would have lasted if they had not received healing ahead of time. Fabio would have come home late from work, tired and hungry, already knowing that their marriage would soon end because no marriage could last very long.

Flor would have been waiting at the door, ready for him, "Where have you been. I know you were out with someone. Who was it this time? And don't try to look so innocent!" Maybe their marriage would have lasted six months.

Flor asked me to speak to another group of women, where I again used her story. After the seminar she told me she had actually forgotten how she had felt back then. When she heard me retell her story she thought, "Yes, that's just how I felt. God healed me so completely I don't even remember the pain."

Were you compared negatively with others? Did they tell you something such as, "John turned out so good, but you aren't worth anything. Did you see how pretty Grace is? But you…" How do you compare yourself with others? Self Forgiveness Sometimes we do things that we ourselves cannot accept and forgive.

We expected something much better from ourselves. We feel humiliated and ashamed of our own shortcomings. Emily was one of these persons.

Emily

EMILY WAS DEPRESSED MOST OF THE TIME. One day she told me about several abortions she had undergone years before. When I asked her whether God had forgiven her, she assured me that He had done so.

"Are you sure God has forgiven you?" I asked again. "Yes, He has forgiven me. I confessed my sins to Him and He promised that He would be faithful to forgive me. I believe He has forgiven me."

"Have you forgiven yourself?"

"Oh, no!" she screamed. "How could I forgive myself for doing something so terrible?"

"Tell me something, Emily" I asked. "Are you holier than God?"

"No," she answered, surprised.

"Aren't you really saying, 'God, you can forgive me. I can accept that. But I am much holier than you are. Because of that I cannot forgive myself.' Isn't this what you are actually saying by accepting God's forgiveness but refusing to forgive yourself?"

"But I killed my babies. They told me they were just a bunch of cells, but I know they were my babies."

"Emily, tell me, where are your babies now?" I asked gently.

"I don't know," she answered sobbing. "That is part of what's so terrible. I think they flushed them down the commode. How could I have done such a terrible thing?"

"Emily, let's ask Jesus to go with you back into your memory to the scene of your first abortion. Imagine yourself taking Jesus by his hand and leading Him to the door of the room. Tell Him everything that you see or hear when you think of that room. Paint Him a word picture of everything that happened and how you felt. Roll everything up in that room, stomp it together and give it to Jesus to carry to the cross. Now see yourself taking that little baby that you know was there, wrap it into a blanket and gently put it into the arms of Jesus. Can you see how He receives it lovingly into his arms?"

"Yes," said Emily. "He receives it so gently and lovingly."

"Ask Jesus to please take care of your baby until you can see it again."

"Jesus," prayed Emily, "I'm so sorry for what I did to my baby. Please take him with you and care for him until I can see him again."

"If you could talk with your baby, what would you want to say to it, Emily?" asked gently.

"Oh," she cried, "I would want to say, 'Please, please, please forgive me. I'm so sorry for what I did to you. I was so tired and had so many children already. I thought I simply couldn't go through having another one. But I am so sorry. I wish I could go back and undo it. I love you. Please forgive me.'"

"Emily," I told her gently, "we cannot talk with your baby. But he is safely with Jesus. Jesus knows where he is right now. Ask Jesus to tell your baby what you would like to say to him."

"Dear Jesus," prayed Emily, "thank you that you are taking care of my baby. Please tell him that I am so very sorry for what I did to him, that I love him very much and I am waiting to see him when I come to heaven."

"Now", I continued, "tell yourself out loud, so that you yourself can hear it, that you forgive yourself with the forgiveness of Jesus."

"Emily," said Emily to herself, "I couldn't forgive you for what you did to your baby, but Jesus has carried what you did to the cross. He has your baby safely in his arms. He is taking care of him. Jesus has poured his forgiveness into me. Emily, I now choose to take Jesus' forgiveness and forgive you for what you did. I forgive and accept you, just as Jesus has forgiven and accepted you."

"And now tell Jesus that you have forgiven yourself with his forgiveness."

"Jesus," prayed Emily, "with your forgiveness I have forgiven myself.

By your grace, I will no longer hold this against myself. I forgive and accept myself, just like you did."

In this way we prayed through her other abortions. "Oh," sighed Emily after we finished, "I feel so much better; like a stone would have fallen from my shoulders."

Take the list you began in the last chapter of all the traumas caused by your father, mother, brothers, sisters, grandparents, aunts, uncles, neighbors, schoolmates, in-laws, husband, wife, pastor, people in your church and by everyone else you can think of and add everything you have done for which you have not been able to forgive yourself.

Also add to the list everything that you reject about your body and your personality. Write the truth because the truth will make you free. Don't write what you think you should write nor what you know you should think. Write what is really in your heart.

Self Acceptance

IN MY FAMILY THERE WERE THREE GIRLS AND a boy when my twin brother and I were born. My four-year-old brother, of course, wanted a brother. But the birth was complicated and since I was born first, my twin brother died.

My older sister, the story teller of our family, told me that the day after we were born, before taking my twin brother to be buried, they put the two babies side by side to see how nearly we looked alike. When my older brother came to see us, he tried to open his new brother's eyes and cried, "No, no! Let the girl die! I don't want another girl! I want my brother to live!"

Things became even worse since I was a rather precocious child. In any group I was always up front, the first to raise my hand when a question was asked, always pushing ahead. My mother would say to me in our Pennsylvania Dutch dialect, "*Sei net so forwitzig*" ("Don't shove yourself ahead so".) But I'd forget and always shoved ahead again.

Somehow, in my child's mind, this shoving ahead and the fact that I was born before my twin brother, joined together. I finally understood that when we were born, I had shoved ahead and caused my brother's death. I had killed him. If I had not been *"forwitzig"* and shoved ahead, he would have been born first and lived, I would have died, and my older brother would have had the brother he so much wanted. I was guilty of the whole thing.

My brother was a mechanic and inventor. Having had no brother to teach his new discoveries, he taught me. For years and years I tried to be a man. But there was no way for me to take the place of the brother I thought I had killed.

I accepted Jesus as my Savior when I was three and a half years old, but I always felt extremely guilty. Although I had done nothing wrong from which I had not repented, my guilty feelings continued.

During my adolescence I felt inferior to everyone. I could not be friends with anyone of the opposite sex. As soon as a boy tried to get to know me better I would say something ugly and cutting to make him leave. I didn't want this; it just happened.

I couldn't understand what was wrong with me until I began my psychiatric studies in nursing school. Finally I understood that I believed I had killed my brother. Unconsciously I felt I was guilty of his death. I was afraid I would kill any man who came close to me. After all, the first boy I ever dated died as the result of an accident. I was a dangerous person!

I was twenty-three years old before I could bring all this to the Lord and be freed from my guilt. Then I finally realized that God had a plan for me in this world as a woman, a plan which no man could fill. My twin brother, or even I as a man, could not have filled this plan. God wanted me, and He wanted me to be a woman. Therefore, He made me as I was and gave me life. He had another plan for my twin brother.

Have you ever accepted yourself just as you are, just as God made you? Have you accepted your sex? Or are you rejecting what God made? Which sex did your parents want their child to be when you were born? Perhaps you are a man but always felt you should be a woman, or you are a woman and always felt you should be a man. How were you treated, or what were you told that makes you feel you should be a man when God made you a woman, or vice versa? Write everything on your list, even the very phrases used, if you can recall them.

We cannot go back into our past and undo things. You cannot go back and erase the words you heard. But Jesus can go into the past and carry the pain they caused. He did not go back and make me die and resurrect my twin brother. But He did carry the pain of the words that I had heard. He carried my feelings of guilt and made me free. I am very happy and content to be a woman. I am happily married and the mother of two adult children and two grandsons.

Your Beginning

PERHAPS YOU FEEL THAT YOUR VERY LIFE IS the result of sin. José was a young man preparing for the ministry. His mother was eighteen and unmarried when he was born. Two weeks after his birth she ran away and left him with his grandparents.

To his grandparents, Jose was only another mouth to feed. He ate too much and cost too much to clothe. He felt he had no right to be alive, since his very beginning was the result of sin. He felt God had no plan for his existence.

Every time Jose spoke in public he had to be fully dressed, complete with vest and tie. He had very little money, but he could not preach without being dressed as elegantly as possible–even beyond his means. Only in this way could he feel worthy to stand before the people. He filled his feelings of inferiority with his well-dressed appearance.

After I spoke to the students about God's healing for psychological wounds, Jose came to pray through his past. I felt led to pray very specifically about his conception.

Yes, his life had begun in a sinful act; we could not deny that. But God had brought his life into being and had kept him from losing it in an abortion or at birth. God had watched over him all through his childhood, preserving his life until that very day because He had a plan for him that only he could fill. Of course the sin was not in his plan, but

Jose was in his plan. I prayed especially that Jesus would carry on himself the sinful act of his parents.

After we finished praying Jose exclaimed, "For the first time in my life I feel that I have the right to exist! Now I see that if God had not wanted me here, He would have taken me in a miscarriage or I just wouldn't have had a beginning. I am here because God had a plan for my life!"

God has a plan for your life. How did your life begin? Have you ever felt that you have no right to live? Tell the truth and add it to your list.

Healing the Sex Life

MANY PEOPLE NEED HEALING IN THE AREA of their sexuality! How many women have been sexually abused or raped, and from then on felt totally dirty and worthless! How many men were victims of homosexual acts or other illicit relations! As a result their concept of sexual relationships is damaged. Some men see women only as objects to be conquered and used. Some women see men only as someone to carry their too heavy boxes and suitcases. Jesus also came to carry these painful experiences to the cross.

María

MARÍA'S STORY SHOWS WHAT GOD CAN DO in the life of a traumatized person. If God could heal María, no one is beyond help, healing or hope.

María was a university student. She had accepted Jesus as her Savior six months before I met her; but she had no peace. A friend asked if I would talk to her. When I met María at the door of my office, her face looked so pale and twisted, so pain-filled that I asked myself what could possibly have happened to her.

María was filled with hatred for her father. He had regularly abused her sexually from the time she was three years old. When her mother sent her to take his early morning coffee to the bedroom, he would close the door and abuse her.

After her eleventh birthday her father stopped bothering her, but then her grandfather, an uncle and two brothers began molesting her. To avenge herself on her father, she began sexual relations with her boyfriend, and later with a second boyfriend. With the third boyfriend she had an abortion. Now she was with her fourth one.

María was furious with everyone. She wanted to kill her father. She was angry with her mother, whom she had tried to tell what was happening and who told her she was lying and had a dirty imagination. María wanted to commit suicide. She was angry with the whole world!

For over half an hour she sat in my office and poured out the horror of what she had lived through. She raved with fury.

What could I possibly say to her? I could only tell her that she was completely right in feeling as she did. She was right in hating her father, her grandfather, her brothers, her uncle and her neighbors, who were suspicious that something was wrong and talked badly about her. Her father called her a prostitute, a loose woman, and wouldn't allow her to leave the house.

I could only tell her, "You're right! Of course, you want to kill your father. You want to commit suicide. You're completely right. Bring out all that fury, all that anger, everything that you feel!"

All I could do was to help her get out her anger. I felt as if the very air were filled with such anger and hatred that I could almost cut it with a knife!

When the girl finally calmed down somewhat, I said to her, "María, you have given your whole life to Jesus, haven't you?"

"Yes," she answered.

"I am going to ask God to open your spiritual eyes so that you can see or imagine Jesus here with us. Can you see Him with your spiritual eyes?"

"Yes, He is here beside me. I can see Him with my inner eyes," answered María.

"Now, let's do something," I continued. "Let's take a big spiritual bag and throw into it, one by one, everything your father did to you, down to the very last thing you told me about. Throw in your hurt, your hatred. Throw in the memory of your father! Tell Jesus that you are throwing everything into His bag."

"Jesus," prayed María, "I take you to the room where I had to take the coffee to my father. I throw into your bag everything he did to me. I throw my father head-first into your bag. I throw in my anger and hatred. I can't handle that anger and hurt. I throw in everything that my grandfather, my uncle and my brothers did to me. I hate them! I throw in that hatred, my humiliation and my dirty feelings." María kept on throwing more and more things into the bag.

"Is there anything else that you can think of to throw into the bag?" I finally asked after she had remained quiet for a while.

"No, nothing that I can think of," she replied.

"Then, María, let's close that bag in the name of Jesus. Jesus," I prayed, "in your name we close this bag. Cover it with your blood. Seal it with the imprint of your nail-scarred hand so that it can never be opened again."

"Now let's you and I, María, take that bag and throw it onto Jesus' shoulders. Can you see Jesus carrying your bag on his shoulder to the cross? It is big and heavy, but He can handle it.

"There He is, hanging on the cross with your bag on his shoulders. What your father did nailed Jesus to the cross. It cost Jesus his life to pay for what your father did to you. And when He dies that bag falls back to hell where it came from and is burned up.

"But Jesus didn't remain dead. He resurrected and comes to you, María. Look deep into Jesus' eyes. See how his love and forgiveness flows to you. Tell Him that you open up that place inside yourself that has been so full of pain, to receive his love and forgiveness, his mercy and peace, and his justification that makes you 'just-as-if' it had never happened. See how He fills that place until it overflows."

"Jesus," prayed María, "I open this place inside of myself that was so filled with hurt. Please fill it with your light, your love, your peace, your forgiveness and your justification. Make me 'just-as-if' this had never happened."

"Now look inside of yourself, María. Can you see Jesus pouring all that love into the place that had been so full of hurt?"

"Yes, He's pouring it all into me," replied María.

"Tell me when it is full and begins to overflow."

After waiting a good while, María finally said, "Now it's full and overflowing."

"Good," I continued. "Now take the forgiveness of Jesus that He is pouring into you, and pass it on to your father. Tell the memory of your father the truth; tell him, 'Father,

I do not have the capacity to forgive what you did to me. I can only hate you. But Jesus has carried the hatred, the hurt and the humiliation to the cross. I now choose to take the forgiveness that Jesus is pouring into me and give it to you, Father. Father, with the forgiveness of Jesus, I choose to forgive you.'"

María was returning to her home that weekend and would need to meet her father. Even after that prayer she felt very frightened. She did not know how she would feel or react when she would see him.

"Don't try to love your father," I told her. "Your father has never given you real love. Therefore you have no love to give him. Just tell the truth. Tell the memory of your father, `Father, I cannot feel love for you, but I open myself up to Jesus so that He can give me his emotions. Whatever He gives me to feel is what I will feel towards you.'" María still felt very frightened.

"Look, María," I finally told her. "You have given your father and all your feelings about him to Jesus. What you feel toward him now is up to Jesus. Don't try to knead your feelings to produce love for him.

"If Jesus doesn't give you anything to feel toward him, don't feel anything. If he gives you indifference, then feel indifference. Just open yourself to Jesus and let Him feel through you. It's his problem now. Go home with confidence, knowing that when you need it, Jesus will put his feelings into you."

María left dreading the encounter. Two weeks later she returned. When she came to the office door I hardly recognized her. Her face had changed so much that I needed some time before I could identify her.

"I cannot say that I love my father," she told me, "but, for the first time in my life I treated him like a person and not like an animal." Now we had to work with the painful memories caused by her mother.

María threw into Jesus' bag everything her mother had done that hurt her, just as she had done with her father. Later we did the same with her grandfather, brothers, neighbors, schoolmates and boyfriends. Each time, we watched Jesus carry the sealed bag to the cross.

When María was unable to forgive, she told the truth: "I cannot forgive. There is no forgiveness in me that can forgive what you did. But, I open myself up to Jesus to receive his forgiveness and I give that forgiveness to you." In this way we worked our way through her whole life, giving the pain to Jesus and forgiving everyone with his forgiveness.

I did not tell María to speak to her father about the past. In spite of this, one day six months later she said, "You know what? Last week I spoke to my father. I had always treated him like an animal. I asked him to forgive me for the way I used to treat him. My father looked at me and said, 'María, please forgive me for what I did to you.'"

Later her father added, "María, you have changed so much. What has happened to you?"

"Jesus has come into my life and changed me," she answered.

"How can Jesus come into my life and change me?" he asked. María wasn't sure what to say, and so she came to ask what she should tell him. She returned to her home to tell him how to become a Christian, but he had abandoned their home the day before she returned.

One year after María's first visit we were ready to leave Colombia for a year. Almost everything in the apartment was packed when María came to visit us. Together we sat on the sofa–the only place left in the house to sit on. "I only came to tell you that I am a woman who is 100% changed," she told me, smiling. "The woman that you see now is not the same one that you met a year ago."

She invited us to her baptism. She would be baptized together with her sister-in-law and her two nephews whom she had led to the Lord.

Later, when we saw María standing in the front of the church ready to be baptized, her face radiant and filled with joy, I remembered the girl who one year before had come to my office with her face pale and twisted, filled with anger and hatred. I thought to myself, "This is the biggest miracle I have ever seen. If God could heal this girl, He can heal anyone!"

The Unwanted Child

MAYBE YOU WERE AN UNWANTED CHILD. Perhaps there were already twelve children in the family and they didn't want a thirteenth one. Or perhaps another child was simply not wanted no matter how small the family, and you were not given the love you needed, as in Karin's case.

Karin

KARIN CAME FROM GERMANY TO SPEND a week with us just to talk about her life. Her parents had planned to have two children. They already had a son and a daughter, and did not want another child. Karin was that third child. Later another son was born.

Karin was born soon after World War II began in Europe. Several times while Karin's father was in the war, her mother, together with the four children, had to flee before the advancing Russian armies. During one of these flights, Karin's little brother and big sister became very ill.

It was near the end of the war, and very few supplies remained in the country. When her mother took the two children to the doctor, he told her that the disease was deadly but he had only enough medication for one child. If she divided it between the two, they would both die. "You must decide which of your two children you will allow to die," the doctor told her.

The mother finally decided to give the medication to her oldest child, Karin's sister. Her little brother died and her mother never forgave herself for his death. Now both girls had to give everything to the remaining brother. They even had to drop their own education and go to work so that their brother could study. It seemed her mother tried to alleviate the guilt she felt for allowing her younger son to die by showering everything on the remaining son. Now, nothing that concerned the girls was important, and especially not for Karin, the extra one.

"You can't do anything right. You're just no good. You spoil everything you touch!" Karin was told over and over.

From the time Karin was a little girl she was given the job of peeling potatoes. If the peelings were too thick, she had to cook them without salt and eat them as a punishment. She was continuously reminded of her unskilled hands.

When Karin was eight years old she ran away from home. She thought she would be missed and someone would come to look for her, showing her that she was loved. But no one came. Since there was no other place to go, she finally had to go back home. No one seemed to have noticed that she had been gone for such a long time.

One year Karin's birthday came while her mother was in the hospital. The children stayed alone with their father. Karin thought, "Today is my birthday. My mother who doesn't love me is in the hospital. Now my father will give me many beautiful gifts."

Since her father was a school teacher, Karin thought he loved children so much that he would surely bring her a great many gifts. In Germany everyone has birthday parties; birthdays are almost as important as Christmas. But Karin's father forgot all about her birthday. Karin had never had a birthday party in all her life.

Many times Karin tried to tell her father how she felt, but he never paid any attention. He was too busy. The school children took up all his time. He had no time left for his daughter.

When Karin told me about her father, I told her, "Tell the memory of your father, 'Father, when you had no time for me, I really felt hurt.'"

But Karin's pain was so deep that she couldn't even say the words. "I tried to speak to my father so many times and he never listened," she groaned. "I know he won't listen. Why should I try again?"

"Tell it to Jesus. He will listen to you," I answered.

"Well, yes, maybe He will listen to me."

"Tell Jesus exactly what they did to you. Give everything to him. You were cruelly punished so often. Give that cruelty to him."

Karin began slowly, "Jesus, they beat me. They told me I was no good. Now, I'm going to tell you that you are no good, Jesus. I'm going to hit you like they hit me. I'm going to beat you just like they beat me!"

Karin began beating the floor and shouting. "Jesus, they hated me; now I hate you! They told me I had to be good. I'm not going to be good! Jesus, I'm going to run away from you. Look! I'm running away! No one came to hunt for me. Now I'm going far away from you!"

Karin screamed and cried and beat the floor, reliving the pain of all the years. It was terrible to hear all the pain that had been piled up inside of her. Had she been the first person that I had helped through her pain, I would have wanted to run away.

For over half an hour Karin continued crying and shouting out her pain. Then suddenly she became quiet. "Jesus, I have done everything to you that they did to me, and you have not gone away. Is there nothing I can do that is so terrible that you will go far away from me? What will make you leave me, Jesus?"

Suddenly she began crying again. "You have taken everything that I have done to you, Jesus, and you just stand there in front of me with your eyes full of love. Oh, Jesus, for the first time in my life I feel your love!"

In the following days and weeks Karin lived through the hurts from her mother, brother, sister, and the other people in her past. She gave them all to Jesus to carry to the cross. Her life began to change radically.

Maybe you were an unwanted child. Is that why you feel the way you do? Tell the truth. The Bible says the truth will make you free.

Telling the truth sounds as though it were such a simple thing to do, but there can be some real obstacles to telling the truth. In the next chapter we will look at some of them.

CHAPTER 6

Obstacles to Telling the Truth

IT IS DIFFICULT TO TELL THE TRUTH about our deepest emotions. Telling the truth opens up parts of our innermost being that we prefer to keep hidden from others and even from ourselves. Expressing them makes us feel exposed and vulnerable. In this chapter, we will look at some of the obstacles that keep us from telling the truth.

Fear of Blaming Others

WHEN WE TELL THE TRUTH ABOUT OUR hurts we may feel that we're blaming others, especially our parents, for our problems. However, telling the truth is not blaming our parents or anyone else. After all, they have their own painful memories from their past experiences, and their parents have painful memories from their past experiences, and so on.

Furthermore, if you are not healed you will pass your traumas on to your children. We cannot act differently from what we are. We will treat our children as we have been treated. Someone must tell the truth and break the chain. This is not blaming anyone.

Who was to blame for my guilt feelings about my twin brother's death? My parents? It wasn't their fault that my brother died. My sister and brother? They didn't know what they were doing. My sister told me the story of my birth with real love. She had no idea of what was happening inside of me. Was I to blame? Certainly not!

To tell the truth about what we feel is not blaming anyone. It is simply telling the story from our point of view. If I were to sit in my office and describe what I would see, I'd say, "There is a very big window with white curtains and brown drapes, and a brown sofa in front of the window."

From where my counselee sits he or she would will say, "There is a brown paneled wall with a green chair in the corner."

I could say, "How can you call that brown sofa a green chair? And those drapes are not paneling!"

My counselee would say, "But don't you see? That chair isn't big enough to be a sofa. And that paneling doesn't look like a window."

I could think, "Wow, there's really something wrong with this person!

He can't even tell the difference between paneling and a window."

We could spend the rest of the day calling each other liars, or trying to define the words "sofa" and "chair." But whoever changed his or her version would end up not telling the truth, because we are both telling the truth about what we see from our own point of view.

When you tell the truth about your painful memories, you will tell what you felt and perceived, not what your parents or brothers and sisters felt and perceived.

If I speak with your parents, your mother will tell one truth, and your father another. Both will be different from your truth because the story will be told from each one's own point of view. We will have three different stories but all will be telling the truth. You must tell your truth, because it is your truth that makes you free. Your father's truth makes him free and your mother's truth makes her free. But only your truth will make you free.

Fear of the Unknown

ANOTHER OBSTACLE TO TELLING THE TRUTH IS fear of the unknown. We may think, "If I begin to tell the truth about what I feel, what will I finally find inside of myself?"

After Karin's healing she said, "Once I told a little bit about my life to a psychologist. It was like opening a little window into my life. There I saw such terrible, black things that I quickly slammed it shut again. I never told her any more.

"I always saw myself like a house with all the doors and windows tightly shut and locked. It was terribly dark inside. Now I see a house with the windows and doors wide open and the sun shining in. Our four children are playing there. The wind is playing with the curtains. But best of all, Jesus is there."

If you begin to tell the truth, you won't know what you will find hidden down underneath everything. Telling the truth hurts; it hurt when you first experienced the pain, and it will hurt when you relive it. But this time it will make you free.

It is not enough just to talk about what happened. You must again feel the pain of what happened. You may cry bitterly about what happened, but unless you open up the actual experience and the pain that you felt, you will remain the same.

To do this you must bring out what you felt when you suffered the incident. What did you feel when you were living through the experience? It is those feelings that we fear. We hurt so much when we lived through the traumatic experience, and now we must re-live those hurts again.

Almost always in the middle of the healing process, when the person is bringing out more and more painful experiences, he will cry, "Is this never going to end? Must I keep on feeling like this for the rest of my life?"

The process will not continue forever. There is an end. But while the person is living through the process it seems as though it were unending. Imagine! If you have lived for twenty or forty years, you have twenty or forty years to clean out before it is over. But there is an end. It will not continue forever.

Karin said, "I have been on a long journey through my life. But now I have finally come home."

The Concept of God

ANOTHER OBSTACLE TO TELLING THE TRUTH IS our concept of God. How is God for you? How does He feel to you? I do not mean the God you know about in your mind, the God about whom you learned all the Bible verses. I mean the God in your heart, deep down in your emotions.

How was your father? Was he very rigid, ready to scold and punish? How was your mother? Was she there for you? It is very interesting that our concept of God, and how we feel about Him, is very similar to our experience with our parents.

It was Sigmund Freud, the "father of psychoanalysis," who said that we project God from the experiences and concepts we have of our earthly fathers. Freud discovered an important truth, but he filtered it through his atheistic mind, and came to the conclusion that God exists only from the projection of our experiences.

It is true that we form our concepts of God from our experiences with our parents, but this does not make God exist. God exists in spite of our projections, not because of them.

Eric Erikson goes a step further in showing how our concepts of God are formed. Erikson believed that a baby, lying in his mother's arms, looks into the mother's face bending over him as though he were looking into a mirror. Erikson believed that from this experience—which every human being must experience in order to survive—awakens the psychological capacity to comprehend the unshakable knowledge that there is a Supreme Being who sees us, even when we are all alone. Atheists would have no God whose existence they could deny if this knowledge of His presence were nonexistent.

Into the baby's world, which consists of himself and his mother's face, says Erikson, comes the father's voice calling the baby's name. This awakens the knowledge in every human being that this Supreme Being calls him, and that He can be heard.

It is the accumulation of these experiences with our parents that paints our emotional picture of what God is like. It is what we see, hear and experience in our homes that forms our basic concepts of God.

God tells us He is like a father who protects us, who is strong and mighty to save. He also tells us that He is like a mother who cannot forget her nursing child, who comforts her child, carrying it in her arms and dandles it on her knees (Isaiah 49:15; 66:12,13). Too often we forget the tender mother images God uses to describe Himself. Yet we long to experience them; to look into his loving face. We pray, "Let the light of your face shine upon us, O Lord" (Psalms 4:6).

God had our whole vocabulary from which He could choose any word He wanted to use to describe Himself. He could have told us He was like a tree. A tree is very nice. When it is hot, the tree provides shade. When it is cold, it gives wood to keep us warm. We can build a house from a tree. It gives fruit to eat. But it isn't a very good friend. I want much more than a tree for my God.

God could have chosen the word "dog" to describe himself. A dog is man's "best friend." It is good to have a dog when one feels alone. A good dog protects his master. But, a dog is also dirty. I'd hate to have a God who is like a dog!

God had our whole vocabulary from which He could choose any words He wanted to tell us what He is like. He chose the words "father" and "mother" because a good father and a good mother describe Him better than any other words in our whole vocabulary.

These words must have described God perfectly while we were in paradise, before the fall of the human race. The child would have seen the tender love and protection, the guidance and correction of his father and mother, and would have known how God was. But the human race fell into sin, and that includes all the fathers and mothers.

Fathers and mothers (biological or surrogate) still portray God to their children. The father is usually the strongest person in the child's whole world.

Mother says, "Wait until Daddy comes. I can't lift it (move it, open it)." To a child, his father can do anything. He is like a god in his small world. The mother is usually the gentlest, most nurturing person in the child's world. A child forms his first concepts of God from his experiences with his father and mother.

But now we are not in paradise. Fathers and mothers no longer portray God correctly. Yet children still learn what God is like from their experiences with their fathers and from what their mothers tell them about their fathers, and from their mothers and from what their fathers tells them about their mothers.

These experiences paint the basic mental and emotional picture of God that each person carries within himself–the picture of how God is, how He acts, and what they can expect of Him. In other words, each person's concept of God has a combination of his father's and mother's virtues and defects. To this basic picture of God, the child's grandparents, neighbors, teachers, pastors and all those in authority add their own versions of what He like. It is through this picture that all the child's, and later the adult's, experiences with God are filtered.

Think for a moment. How is your God? How was your father? What was your mother like? I remember very well when God showed me that I was talking to Him in the same way my mother had talked to my father.

I was born into a very good, Christian family. We were all carried to church in our parents' arms. Their most fervent desire was to see their children follow the Lord. All of us are serving the Lord in one way or another.

My mother came from a family of generations of pastors, missionaries, musicians and school teachers, but to some degree she always felt inferior to her ten brothers and sisters. She thought she couldn't sing as well as the rest, nor was she a teacher. She was "just" an artist, and painting in her mind was not as important as singing and teaching.

My father came from a "down to earth" family of generations of farmers. The only books he read were his Bible and commentary. He wanted to run our farm just like his father and grandfather had done and changed only in the later years of his life. My mother, however, wanted to farm according to the latest agricultural and horticultural scientific discoveries.

Although my parents loved each other dearly, my mother could never quite accept my father as he was. In her fear of being found below par, she constantly tried to make my father meet her high goals by telling him, "You should do this or that. Now don't forget to . . . . Be sure you . . ., etc., etc."

After of my parents had died and I was preparing to leave for the mission field, one day, God stopped me when I was praying and said, "Arline, you are talking to Me exactly the way your mother that talked to your father."

I couldn't believe what I had heard! I wanted to hide my head under my pillow! I didn't like the way my mother had talked to my father. There were many, many very good things about my mother that I wanted to learn, but not the way she had told my father what to do.

Then I heard God laughing; not a nasty kind of laugh—just a kind, friendly little chuckle. "Arline," He asked, "did you think I didn't know this all along? I was just waiting for you to realize it and admit the truth so that you would let me do something about it."

Then God showed me how I had been praying. I prayed, more or less, "Dear Lord, please do this and that. Please don't let this or that happen. If you don't want to do it that way, God, it's OK, but I think it would be better this way. Dear Lord, please this and that and the other."

I never prayed, "Lord, show me what you want me to do. I know you want the best for me. Just show me what you want and I'll do it, because you know the end from before the beginning. You know the best way to get to what is good for me. I choose to trust you even though I don't understand the way you are leading me."

At last I had to admit it. "Yes, Lord, it's the truth. I do talk to you the way my mother talked to my father. And what's more, I'm not at all sure that you even know what's best for me if I don't tell you how things are going down here. That you are good and love me and are always there for me, I clearly know. But I simply don't feel or believe that you really understand what's best if I don't tell you how things look to me." When I finally admitted the truth, God began to change me and my prayers.

For some of us, the mental and emotional picture of God makes trusting him virtually impossible. Theresa's story shows how her childhood experiences gave her a picture of God that filled her with terror.

Theresa

THERESA WAS PREPARING FOR THE MINISTRY, but when she prayed she could never close her eyes and the door to her room had to remain open. Otherwise, she felt as if a ghost were creeping up behind her, getting ready to grab her. It took us two months to discover the reason.

Theresa's father had studied to be a pastor, but wandered far away from God. He became an alcoholic. He was in jail when she was born. He finally abandoned his family when she was six years old.

As a child Theresa feared that some day her father would return and carry her away to some dark, ugly room filled with empty beer bottles, without any flowers or anything beautiful. This became a terror that constantly haunted her life.

Later Theresa became a Christian, but she could never tell God about her real feelings. She could ask him for things, such as a pair of shoes, but could never express her emotions. Slowly it became clear that to Theresa, God was like a ghost–just a bunch of bones covered with a sheet. If she were to close the door when she prayed, God might appear in the room with her and then anything could happen! Maybe He would even spirit her far away to some terrible place.

"Theresa," I said to her one day, "tell God the truth. Tell Him, 'God, I'm scared of you.'"

Theresa began praying, "God, thank you because you love me, thank you for what you did for me, thank you for this, thank you for that. . . ."

I interrupted her prayer, "No, not that way. Just say, 'God, I'm scared of you.'"

"God, thank you for this, thank you for that...," she prayed again.

Again I interrupted, "Only pray, 'God, I'm scared of you.'"

Eventually she managed to say, "God . . . I'm . . . scared . . . of you, but I should be, because you are so big and I'm so little!"

"No, no! Not like that," I repeated. "Simply pray, 'God, I'm scared of you.' Nothing more."

Again she began, "God . . . I'm . . . scared . . . of you, but, I've reason to feel like that, God, because I'm here all alone!"

Theresa continued struggling with that prayer for a long time before she could calmly admit to God that she was afraid of Him. She hadn't been able to admit the truth because if God really knew how she felt He would surely come and get her. And who could guess what He would do with her!

We had to return to Colombia before I could give Theresa all the time she needed. Before leaving, I asked her how God seemed to her then. She had begun to close the door to her room and could even close her eyes if she wanted to when she prayed. She was beginning to develop more confidence with Him. He was becoming less like her father.

What does God feel like to you? Tell the truth. The truth will make you free! Take the list of all your painful memories and add your concept of God. Write down what you really feel about him. Add anything that God permitted to come into your life that makes you feel hurt and angry at Him and are unable to forgive, such as the fact that your parents divorced, that your brother died, or anything else that comes into your mind.

In the next chapter we will look at some other factors that are essential to our emotional healing.

CHAPTER 7

The Occult and the Decision for Christ

Another obstacle that can hinder our emotional healing is a previous contact with the occult.

God has put into each of us the capacity to come into contact with the supernatural world. He made us in this way so that we can have communion with himself. However, there are two supernatural worlds: the kingdom of Light, ruled by God, and the kingdom of Darkness, ruled by Satan. Ever since the human race fell into sin we have been able to make contact with both supernatural worlds.

If someone has had contact with the occult in any form, he has been in contact with that which is detestable to God. God said:

Let no one be found among you... who practices divination or sorcery, interprets omens, engages in witchraft, or casts spells, or who is a medium or spiritist or who consults the dead; anyone who does these things is detestable to the Lord (Deut. 18:10-12)

All these practic are detestable to God. If you want Jesus to heal your painful memories, you must renounce and reject every contact you may have had with these practices.

Although people who practice these things do have real power, their power does not come from God. They have used the powers from the Kingdom of Darkness. People who practice these abominations, or consult someone who practices them, open themselves to the kingdom of Satan. We can describe this as something similar to making a telephone contact or to opening a door to Satan's kingdom. We might illustrate this in the following way:

<Insert Image 11>

Later these people accept Jesus as their Savior and try to do God's will. In spite of this, the contact made with the kingdom of Satan continues. Satan does not give up his territory willingly.

When reading the Bible and praying, it is very difficult to concentrate. Such persons feel hindered when they want to go to church or to pray. Often they have basic doubts about God's love, or even about His very existence, which intrude into their minds. They may feel that God is unfair or a liar.

As long as the contact made with the kingdom of Satan has not been broken, we can compare our relationship with the supernatural world with trying to hold a telephone conversation with the wires crossed. If two conversations are being held simultaneously, no one can understand anything. It could be illustrated in the following way:

<Insert Image 12>

When the person renounces, in the name of Jesus, all contact he or she has had with the occult and closes all doors that were opened to the kingdom of Satan, the connection to Satan's kingdom is broken. We can illustrate this in the following way:

<Insert Image 13>

There are people who say, "Yes, I went to a place like that, but I really didn't believe in it. I just accompanied a friend." That makes no difference. The Bible tells us that Satan is like a thief. No thief waits to enter a house until the owner believes he is a thief. No thief comes to the door, knocks, and says, "I am a thief. Please let me come in. I want to rob you." Such a thief would die of starvation!

A thief enters when the doors and windows are believed to be tightly locked. This is how Satan works. He does not wait to come until we invite him. He comes when we least expect him—when we least believe he's around. Luz Angela's story shows us the far reaching effects even innocent contacts with the occult can have.

Luz Angela

Luz Angela had been a Christian for many years. Her husband was a pastor. For years she fought against doubts about her salvation. She doubted that God really loved her. She fasted and prayed many times because of these doubts, but they never diminished.

In a seminar, my husband talked about the need to renounce all contact with any kind of spiritism and to close any door that was opened to the kingdom of Satan. This goes a step beyond merely repenting of the act.

Later, in a group meeting, Luz Angela told me about her doubts. In her junior year of high school, she had feared that she would fail a final examination. A friend told her to go to the cemetery where a very wicked man had been buried the day before and find a candle end that had remained on his grave. She should light the candle, and hold it firmly in both hands while she knelt by the grave and repeated the "The Lord's Prayer" backwards.

Luz Angela did everything exactly as she had been told. Later she forgot all about the incident. Now she wondered if this could possibly be the root of her doubts.

Luz Angela renounced this occult ritual in the name of Jesus. In His name she closed the door that had been opened in her life to the kingdom of Satan. Later Luz Angela told us that from that day she had been free of her doubts. Never before had she experienced such freedom.

Have you been in contact with the occult? How about your parents and grandparents? Exodus 20:5 tells us that these effects and influences can continue to the third and fourth generations.

Right now make a list of any contact you may have had with the occult. Also write down anything you may know of such contacts that your parents or grandparents may have had.

Accepting Jesus as Your Savior

IF YOU WANT JESUS TO HEAL YOUR PAINFUL memories, you must first permit Him to enter into your life and have access to every part. Without giving Him the right to enter into your life, it is impossible for Him to heal you, as the following story shows.

Some time ago we had a leaking pipe in our kitchen. We called a plumber to come and fix it. Suppose that, when the plumber knocked on the door of our apartment, we had told him he could not come inside because the apartment belonged to us; that he should fix the pipe by stretching his arms in through the door or the window. I assure you that the water would still be dripping! Repairing the pipe would have been totally impossible!

The same is true if you want Jesus to heal the painful memories in your life. He cannot do so if you do not open your life to Him and give Him access to every part.

You may say, like many people have told me, "But God has always been with me." This is true; God has always been with you. But He has always been with the cats and the dogs and the trees and all of His creation. He wants a much closer relationship with us humans.

Genesis chapter two tells us that when God formed Adam out of the dust of the ground, He breathed into him the breath of life and Adam became a living being. Later God told Adam and Eve that if they were to eat from the tree of the knowledge of good and evil they would surely die.

They ate but did not die; they continued to live. However, the Greek word which we translate "to die" does not mean "to terminate." It means rather, "to separate." When the body dies, there is a separation between the body and the soul. We see this when the body becomes lifeless.

At the moment that Adam and Eve ate of the tree of good and evil, a separation took place in them. The breath of life that God had breathed into them separated from them;

it departed. A separation took place between God and them. They died spiritually.

This separation has come all the way down to us. This is why we feel so empty inside. It is an emptiness so big and so deep that we cannot fill. We try to fill it with cars, houses, money, clothes, jobs, family, children, companions, friends and much more. But it is much too deep to be touched by any of these things because it is a God-sized, God-shaped emptiness in our spirit. Only God in Jesus Christ, through the Holy Spirit, can fill this emptiness of our spirit.

How can Jesus enter one's spirit and fill the emptiness? He tells us in Revelation 3:20, "Here I am! I stand at the door and knock; if anyone hears my voice, and opens the door, I will enter in and eat with him and he with me."

If I would knock at the door of your house and you wanted me to enter, you would open the door and invite me to come in. If I were welcome, you would invite me into the living room. If you wanted me to eat with you, you would invite me to be seated at your table. But if you wanted me to become the owner of your house, you would take me through the house and show me everything.

You would say, "This is your house. It belongs to you. Tell me what I shall do with it. What color do you want me to paint this room? Just tell me what you want and I will do it."

This is what must happen in your life with Jesus. Jesus is not a thief. He respects you and your choices. He is a gentleman. He will not enter anywhere without an invitation. He stands at the door of your life and knocks. If you open your life to Him, He will enter, but not without an invitation.

How can you invite Jesus to enter into your life? In the same way that you would ask me to come into your house: with a verbal invitation. Invite Him to come into your life with the following prayer guide.

Prayer Guide: "Lord Jesus, I realize that I have never opened my life to you. You have always been with me, but I have never invited you to come into my life. Here and now, I give to you my whole self. I open the door of my life to you. I ask you to come in and forgive my sins.

"Lord Jesus, I want to belong to you. Forgive everything that I have done against you and against others. Make me a child of God. Tell me what you want me to do with my life, and I will do it. I want you to be Lord of my life. Thank you for what you are doing in me. Amen."

Renouncing the Occult

NOW RENOUNCE ALL CONTACT THAT YOU HAD with the detestable things of the occult. Take your list and renounce everything, one by one. You may use the following prayer as a guide:

Prayer Guide: "Lord God, I here and now renounce, in the name of Jesus of Nazareth, every contact that I had with anything that is detestable to you. I renounce and reject all religions that do not acknowledge You. I renounce all contact with divination and sorcery, all witchcraft and casting of spells, all mediums or spiritists, all consulting with the dead. I renounce all use of tarot cards and Ouija boards, all palm reading, all kinds of fortune telling, all astrology and reading of horoscopes.

I also renounce all lying, gossip, drunkenness, and use of drugs. I renounce all contact with any of these things that my parents may have had. I close all doors that this has opened to the kingdom of Darkness. Lord Jesus, I renounce all this and separate myself from everything. I pray that you will clean all the areas of my life that have been affected and fill them with your Holy Spirit."

If there is something left on your list that you have not mentioned, bring it to Jesus in the same way.

Prayer Guide: "In the name of Jesus, I, here and now, renounce and close the door that was opened in my life to the kingdom of Satan when I was in contact with _____ when I went to _____, and when I used (or did) _____. Please fill with the Holy Spirit every part of my life that these contacts have affected. Thank you, Lord God, for delivering me."

In the next chapter you will find prayer guides that you may use to bring your own or another person's painful memories to Jesus for healing.

CHAPTER 8

Prayer Guides for Healing

I N THIS CHAPTER YOU WILL FIND PRAYER guides that you may follow in order to bring your emotional wounds and painful memories to Jesus for healing. Ask God to open your spiritual eyes so that, in your mind's eye, you can see or imagine Jesus there with you. Ask Him to guide you back through the years of your life.

Show Jesus every scene in your life that has left you traumatized. Ask Him to hold out an open bag into which you can throw everything that has hurt you. Roll up every scene, fold it over, stomp it into little pieces like ashes and throw it into his bag. Then ask Him to enter the scene and give you something beautiful to remember. Ask Him to show you what He would have done if He had come in at the moment when everything happened.

In order to do this, you may use the following prayer as a guide. Fill in the spaces with the memories and emotions of your wounds and traumas.

Prayer Guide: "Lord Jesus, when _____
_____ _____ *(e.g., my father made me*

go out alone when I was so scared, etc.), I felt _____ *(e.g., terribly angry, etc.).* I wanted to _____ *(e.g., scream until he would listen and understand me, etc.)* but he _____ *(e.g., wouldn't listen to me, etc.).* Lord Jesus, this _____ *(e.g., fear and anger)* is destroying me. I cannot carry it any longer. I cast this _____ *(e.g., fear and anger, etc.)* into your bag. Thank you for carrying this for me."

When everything from the first painful experience is in the bag, go on to the second one and fill in the spaces with that one. Tell the truth about what you felt then and add what you feel now. Scream, cry, beat the floor or pillow if you feel like doing so; free those emotions so that you can feel them again and throw them into Jesus' bag. If you both love and hate your father throw your memories of him into the bag and ask Jesus to filter out the good ones and return those to you. He can filter them much better than you can sort them out.

When you have finished with all the painful memories of your father, continue with those of your mother. Then continue with all the hurts caused by your brothers and sisters, naming each of them in turn.

Then continue with the painful memories caused by your step-father, step-mother, aunts and uncles, grandfathers and grandmothers, cousins, neighbors, schoolmates, teachers, boyfriends, girlfriends, people with whom you worked, professors, counselors, pastors, people in the church, missionaries, mother-in-law, father-in-law, all the other in-laws, husband, wife, ex-husband or ex-wife, sons, daughters, and anyone else you can think of.

Now do the same with the painful memories you caused yourself–those things you cannot forgive and accept about yourself.

Now tell God everything that you have felt towards Him; tell Him what you have not been able to forgive.

> ***Prayer Guide:*** "God, I have always felt that you were _____ _____ *(e.g., cold and distant, etc.)*, that you are_____ *(e.g., unfair, etc.)*. I have never been able to forgive the fact that you allowed _____ *(e.g., my brother to die, etc.)*. I have felt _____ *(e.g., very angry, etc.)* with you, God. But now I throw all this into Jesus' bag. I take this emotional picture that I have of You, God, and tear it to pieces and throw it into Jesus' bag. God, if you aren't like the picture that I have of you, then I don't know how or who you are. Please show me how you really are."

If you have been unable to trust Jesus or have felt afraid of Him, tell the real, kind, loving Jesus who carried your sins to the cross—that Jesus who you know lives deep within you—how you usually or sometimes feel about Him. Throw all that into Jesus' bag.

When you cannot think of any other hurtful scene or emotion to throw into the bag, tell Jesus, "Lord Jesus, if there is something else to throw into the bag that I cannot remember, please bring it back to my memory now so that I can give it to you."

Remain quiet before Him for a while. If anything, no matter how small or large, comes to your mind, relive the pain and throw it into the bag. If nothing comes to your mind, thank Him for the things that He has shown you and then continue your prayer:

> ***Prayer Guide:*** "Jesus, in your name I close this bag. Cover it with your blood and seal it with the imprint of your nail-scarred hand, so that it can never be opened again. And now I throw that big, heavy bag onto your shoulder to carry to the cross for me.
>
> "Jesus, you are walking to the cross, bent down under the weight of my bag. Thank you for carrying it for me. You are nailed to the cross with my bag on your shoulders. And there from the cross, that bag falls back into hell where it all came from, and is consumed. Jesus, those hurts that I suffered caused your death. You died to pay for what I suffered. Thank you so much.
>
> "Thank you that you come to me, now resurrected. In your eyes I see your love, compassion, forgiveness, mercy and your justification that makes me `just-as-if' all this had never happened. I open myself up to you to receive your healing, your love, your compassion, your forgiveness, your justification."

Now turn to the memory of your father and tell him the truth. "Father,

I could not (or only half) forgive you for what you did to me. I did not have the forgiveness in me to give to you. But now I have thrown everything to Jesus' bag and He carried it to the cross. It cost Jesus his life to pay for what you did to me. He is pouring his forgiveness into me. Father, I now choose to take the forgiveness of Jesus and give it to you. With his forgiveness I forgive what you did to me, Father. By the grace of God, I will no longer hold this against you.

Forgive me for the wrong ways in which I acted toward you, and the times I hurt you." Now tell Jesus what you did.

> *Prayer Guide:* "Jesus, I couldn't forgive my father. But now I have chosen to give your forgiveness to him. With your forgiveness, Jesus, I forgive my father. By your grace and power I will no longer hold this against him."

In the same way, give the forgiveness of Jesus to your mother, your sisters, your brothers, and everyone else on your list.

> *Prayer Guide:* Now forgive yourself with the forgiveness of Jesus. Write in your own name: "_____ , I could not forgive you for _____. But now I have given this to Jesus and I forgive you with the forgiveness of Jesus. I choose to accept you just as you are, with your defects and your strong points, just as Jesus accepted you."

Tell Jesus that you have forgiven yourself. Tell him, "Jesus, I have chosen to forgive myself and accept myself just as you have forgiven and accepted me."

Now tell God how you feel about Him.

> *Prayer Guide:* "God, I have never been able to forgive you for allowing _____ *(e.g., my parent's divorce, etc.)*. But now I have given all that to Jesus to carry to the cross and with His forgiveness, I forgive this. I will not hold this against you anymore. Please forgive my attitude toward you. Show me how you really are. Lord Jesus, show me God the Father. I want to know Him as He really is. I want to know Him

like you knew Him when you were here on earth."

If nothing else comes to your mind that needs to be taken care of, finish this prayer time by thanking God for the miracle of healing He is bringing about in you.

Living with Daily Trauma and Anxieties

EVEN THOUGH YOU MAY NOW BE FREE of the pain of memories of your past, the time will come when something new will happen that hurts you. Do not deny that what the person said or did hurts you. Tell the truth. Don't try to forget it. Remember the scene. Remember how you felt. Walk into the pain with Jesus. Maybe you don't really know what you felt. Ask God to show you what you felt; then tell Him the truth.

When your husband comes home angry, or your wife is cranky, admit to Jesus exactly how you feel. "I am _____ *(e.g., angry and hurt, etc.)* I feel like _____ *(e.g., ringing his/her neck, etc.).*"

If that is how you feel, admit the truth. There is no problem with feeling that way. The problem begins when you respond to the feeling in a wrong way. The Bible says, "Be angry, but sin not." (Ephesians 4:26, KJV) Our feelings of anger are no problem for God since Jesus came to carry them to the cross. The problems arise from our attitude towards our anger. If we try to hide what we feel, we are in trouble. If we punch the person in the nose, we are also in trouble.

Too often we pray, "God, forgive me for my anger," and then swallow both the anger and the pain that caused the anger. If, day after day, we swallow more pain and anger, we will become so tightly filled up inside that the smallest thing will make us explode. If we do not tell the truth, God cannot free us from the angry feelings. Tell Jesus the truth.

> ***Prayer Guide:*** "Lord Jesus, when _____ said _____ I felt _____ and I still feel _____ *(e.g., angry, hurt, belittled, etc).* I am angry at him/her for _____. I cannot carry this anger and hurt. I give you everything that happened, together with this anger and hurt. Please carry it to the cross and fill me with your peace. Give me your forgiveness for him/her. In your name, Jesus, I choose to give your forgiveness to _____."

Every person should daily bring his or her hurts to God for healing in order to keep them from accumulating and weighing him or her down.

Praying for Others

SOME PEOPLE'S LIVES HAVE BEEN ONE long, continual hurt. In such cases it is helpful to pray through the person's whole life. This prayer may be used as a guide to pray through one's own life, through someone else's life on a one-to-one basis, or by a leader praying with a group.

Put your name or the name of the person being prayed for in the spaces of the following prayer. As you lead the person or group in prayer, have them follow the prayer, forming mental pictures and feeling the emotions of what you are praying. Their eyes and ears saw and heard, and their bodies and emotions felt the tragic things when they happened, now they need to see, hear and feel the resolutions that God wants to give them. Ask Jesus to take the people's hands and guide them through their lives as you pray. The prayer is written in the masculine in order to distinguish the one being prayed for from the feminine pronoun of the mother.

Prayer Guide: "Lord Jesus, I thank you that with you there is no past.

Everything is present. I pray that you would take _____ *(e.g., my, Joe's or each person's)* hand and walk with him back through his life. Go with him to his youth, his childhood, the day of his birth and all the way back to the day of his conception.

"Lord, free _____ from all negative influences that came to him from the life of his parents, grandparents and great-grandparents. We, renounce in the name of Jesus, any witchcraft or spiritism in which they may have taken part, or any spell that was cast or pact that was made before _____ was conceived. In your name we renounce and annul these and close the door to the Kingdom of Satan that may have been opened in his life. Fill every part of his life that was affected from all this with your Holy Spirit.

"Lord Jesus, look at the moment of the conception of _____. Perhaps it was a moment of deep love, maybe it was an unplanned accident, or possibly there was sin involved. Jesus, enter into this moment and make of that act something beautiful as you intended it to be. If there was sin, please forgive and cleanse everything. Lord Jesus, you are in control of everything; you wanted this life to begin. You had a plan for _____ before the foundation of the world was laid. Thank you for your plan and for his life.

"Jesus, when the mother first realized that she was expecting a baby, perhaps she became frightened.

Possibly even at that very early moment of his life _____ was rejected. Lord Jesus, come to that mother's side and comfort her. Give her such joy and confidence in you that even the baby will feel it.

"Perhaps the mother had a difficult pregnancy or became ill. Perhaps she was not married and felt guilty. Lord, I pray, take those sicknesses, that guilt, and heal any trauma they may have caused in the baby.

"Lord Jesus, when the time comes for delivery, I ask that you go to that mother's side. Possibly the delivery was long and difficult. Reach out and carry her pain. Keep the baby from all trauma.

"When _____ is born, receive him into your arms. May your radiant face be the first to welcome him into this world. Tell him that you love him and are very happy that he has been born. Consecrate him even now to the work of your kingdom.

"Lord Jesus, during those first days and years when a baby has such great need for a mother's care, perhaps when he needed her to hold and rock him and give him security, she was too busy to care for him in the way that he needed. Maybe because of poverty, illness or death, _____ _____ was separated from his mother and left alone or with someone who could not care for him properly.

"Jesus, please go into the place where _____ is crying, hold him in your arms, change his diapers, give him his bottle, rock him gently in your arms. Tell him that you love him and will provide for all his needs.

"When he is a little older and enters the "no" stage and later asks so many questions, perhaps his mother becomes impatient and angry, and tells him to shut up and to ask no more questions. Perhaps he even begins to learn not to talk about what he thinks and feels. Lord Jesus, take this child into your lap, snuggle him into your arms, listen to all his questions and give him the answers he needs. Heal any trauma he may have received when he felt rejected.

"Lord Jesus, maybe during those years his father or mother had no time for _____, or perhaps they were very brusque with him. I ask that you take that child into your strong arms and be a father and a mother to him. Make _____ feel your protection and care.

"Perhaps the father (or mother) was an alcoholic and mistreated the mother (or child) with words or even beat her. Come into the room with that frightened family—perhaps the children are hiding under the bed in terror. Lord Jesus, please go in there and confront his father (or mother). Let that beating, those ugly words, that abuse, that negligence fall on you. Bring that family out of there without any remaining painful memories, just because you are there. Put your hand over the wounds that _____ received during that time and heal him completely. Fill him with your love and confidence. Thank you because you are doing this.

"Jesus, in the years following his early childhood there were times when _____, being a child, acted in a way that needed punishment. Possibly his parents, instead of teaching him with love and understanding, ridiculed and criticized him and made him feel that he couldn't do anything right. Perhaps they never or seldom praised him and now he feels insecure and inferior to others. He may think he will always fail.

"Lord Jesus, walk with _____ and tell him when he has done things well. Tell him you are very proud of the way he is developing and learning. Explain to him everything he needs to know. When he misbehaves and needs to be punished, you punish him correctly in love. Explain to him the reason for his punishment. When he was punished unjustly, cover him with yourself and take that punishment in your body. Perhaps there were times when his older brothers and sisters did not understand _____. Perhaps they ridiculed and demeaned him. Take the pain of those wounds and heal them.

"Lord, when _____ began going to school, perhaps everything seemed strange and new to him. Possibly he was scared. Take his hand and go to school with him. Possibly the other children pushed him aside at times or bullied him and made him feel alone and unwanted. Perhaps a teacher made him feel worthless and stupid or even made fun of him. Stay with _____ and be his best friend. Take those hurts on yourself and let him go free. Thank you because you are doing this.

"Lord Jesus, when _____ became an adolescent possibly no one explained the facts of life to him. Perhaps everything came to him as a surprise, causing fear and shame. Possibly his own experimentations still makes him feel guilty. Lord Jesus, please go to him in his memories and explain everything to him. Take his fear, shame, insecurity and guilt on yourself.

"Perhaps _____ was molested or raped and since then has felt dirty and worthless. Or perhaps _____ was taken to a brothel or molested by some homosexual person. Jesus, enter into those scenes and clean out the mind, emotions and body of _____, wash him in the water of your righteousness and make him just as clean as if it had never happened. Thank you for what you are doing.

"Perhaps a special friend of _____ cheated on him and now it is impossible for him to confide in the love of the opposite sex. Please, Lord, carry this pain on yourself."

If you use this prayer to pray to help someone pray through his life, he may experience great pain. Allow him to express that pain in whatever way he is able to bring it out. Remember, there is nothing too big for God to heal. Take time to stay with him until the pain has subsided and he is quiet again. Help him to bring a list of any unmentioned painful memories to Jesus, following the prayer guide at the beginning of this chapter. If the list is too long or is he is very tired, allow him to continue the following day or week. Finish the prayer time with a time of praise for what God is doing and has done in his life.

Most people feel exhausted after such an intense time of prayer. Encourage the person to take time to rest and reflect over what is taking place in his life. Some will need a time to grieve over what they experienced. Encourage the person to take all the time he needs to work through any additional memories that may surface later on.

In the next two chapters we will examine some of the things we need to do in order to retain our emotional healing.

CHAPTER 9

Remaining Healed

In the last chapter you prayed through your life. How do you feel now? It may be that the pain of your memories is gone. It may be that you are not quite sure if it's gone. If you are not sure, do not say that everything is okay, because it is the truth that will make you free. If you are not sure, ask God to show you if you have something painful is still repressed.

Some people while praying see their whole life pass before their eyes, like a video. Others don't see anything. Some say they saw only a black hole. Others experience variations between these extremes all mixed together.

Whatever you experienced, that is where God will meet you. If you saw your whole life pass before you and the pain is gone, thank Him for that. If you didn't experience anything, then ask Jesus to show you what He wants your next step to be. If you saw only a black hole, then bring that black hole to Jesus. Give Him permission to bring his light into the darkness and to show you what makes it so dark. Then go quietly about your duties, expecting that when you can understand Him, God will show you what you need to bring to Him.

You have been healed just as far as you were able to open up and tell God the truth. However, God knows just how much you can bear to bring to Him at one time. Possibly all you could handle, and all He showed you, was the first layer. After a time of quiet, He will take you to a deeper level.

Just remain quietly before Him as you go about your daily tasks and He will show you what that deeper level is. Choose to trust Him. He will lead you gently. He wants to heal you more than you can ever want to be healed. If you seem to come to a dead end, ask God to lead you to a good Christian counselor who can help you understand what He is trying to show you.

If you feel that everything on your list has been healed, then burn your list. Do not keep the list, because Jesus has carried that pain away. Nothing on that list belongs to you anymore. The pain and shame of every memory now belongs to Jesus. They are his property.

If later on Satan tries to tell you, "But, do you remember what they did to you?" you can answer, "On October 24 (put in your own date) I put all that on Jesus. I saw Him carry it to the cross. I have nothing to do with it anymore. If you want to talk about that you go talk to Him. That is no problem of mine. It doesn't belong to me and I do not meddle in other people's business! Jesus, thank you that you carried that to the cross for me. Thank you that I am free."

Thought Habits

JESUS HAS COME TO MAKE US FREE FROM OUR emotional wounds and painful memories, but how do we remain free?

How can we keep from digging around in the place where the wound had been?

The Bible tells us in Romans 12:2 (KJV) that we need to be "transformed by the renewing of your mind." This is very important if we want our emotional healing to remain intact.

We human beings develop patterns of thought. When we remember someone, we also remember the feelings the person produced in us. The fact that I could not do my work well in the presence of my Nursing Arts instructor who looked like my third grade teacher shows that I had developed a habit of thinking. Every time I saw that type of features my mind thought "fear… failure… punishment." Those thoughts constantly dug around in the wounds that my third grade teacher had caused. That kind of thinking had to be changed.

Perhaps you have tried to break some habit such as smoking or using bad language. You know that the habit is not broken from one day to the next. It takes a real battle to break a habit.

It also takes a real battle to break our thought patterns. The more firmly a habit has developed, the harder it will be to break. Thought patterns are not broken simply by saying, "I won't think about that anymore."

An interesting thing about our thought processes is that in order to say that we will forget something, we must first remember what we say we will forget. When we say, "I won't think about that anymore," we have already broken our resolve.

Do an experiment. Carefully carry out the following instruction: Do not think of bread. Don't think about how bread smells when it comes out of the oven, or how good bread tastes. What are you thinking of? Of bread, of course! The more we try to forget thinking about bread, the more we remember it.

Our thoughts are like glue. We pick it all off from one hand only to find it sticking to the other hand. Then we pick it all off the other hand and it sticks to the first. We cannot get rid of it. So, too, are our thoughts. The more we try to forget, the more we remember.

God knows that our thoughts work like this and He gave us the solution to this dilemma. This solution we find in Philippians 4:8.

Finally, brothers, whatever is true, whatever is noble, whatever is right, whatever is pure, whatever is lovely, whatever is admirable—if anything is excellent or praiseworthy—think about such things.

Read the verse again and see how many of the things we shall think about are negative. There is not one negative thing in the whole verse; all are positive. We should fill our minds by thinking on positive things. This is a command of God, not just a suggestion. His command is: Think on these positive things.

God knows how He made us. He knows that the only way we can change the empty way of thinking or living which we received from our fathers (1 Peter 1:18) is by filling our minds with good thoughts.

It is difficult to keep our minds filled with good thoughts. When we see someone who has hurt us, the first thing that comes to our minds is, "Remember what he did!?"

Thoughts that do not fit into Philippians 4:8 come into the category of thoughts that we are told in II Corinthians 10:3-6 to take captive and bring into obedience to Christ

Jesus. We must replace these negative, damaging thoughts with good thoughts.

Very carefully do another experiment: Do not think of bread. Don't think about how bread smells when it comes out of the oven, or how good fresh bread tastes. Think of water. Think of the sparkling coolness of water on a hot day and how the water refreshes you. What are you thinking of? If you did the experiment carefully you will be thinking of water. The second thoughts displaced the first.

I have met only one person who always talked of the good in others. If she knew nothing good to say about someone, she didn't say anything. When a conversation brought out something negative in a person she always managed to steer the conversation around until some good trait in the person was noticed. Being with her was a beautiful experience.

This friend, a missionary, took care of us when I had cancer surgery. She stayed with us for a whole week. When she returned to her home, another missionary came to replace her for one week.

This second missionary was almost the exact opposite of the first one. She saw everything and everyone in a very negative light. After a week I could hardly wait until she left. It was very depressing to constantly hear of all the terrible things everyone had done.

Both of these women had developed thought habits. They spoke about the same people and events. Yet, because of the thought habits each had developed, they saw the exact opposite in everyone and every situation.

The Little Old Grandmother

SOMETIMES IT IS HARD TO FIND SOMETHING good in someone. Perhaps we all need to learn from a little old grandma who lived in a country village. This little old lady always looked for the good in others. She had Philippians 4:8 written over her mind.

In the same village lived a crotchety old man. One day the old man died. Since it was a small village everyone went to the funeral. After the burial some boys decided to have a bit of fun at the old grandmother's expense.

"Now, Grandma," they asked her, "what can you tell us about this old man who just died?"

The little old grandmother scratched her head and said nothing for a while. Finally, after much thought, she replied, "You know, I've always said that man had the most beautiful teeth in the whole world!"

Perhaps in your life someone has hurt you so deeply that you feel there is nothing good about him or her. Perhaps after much searching the only good thing you can find are his "beautiful teeth." Then, after you bring your hurts to Jesus, fill your mind with thoughts of his "beautiful teeth."

Every person has something good about him or her. Everyone has the image of God hidden somewhere inside of him or herself. We must concentrate on finding the good. It is the only way to be freed from negative thoughts and to break the thought patterns we have developed.

I challenge you to search out the good qualities in the person who has hurt you. When you realize that you are thinking negative thoughts, cast them on Jesus and focus on the person's good qualities. This does not mean that you deny what he or she did. Rather, it means that you focus on the fact that since you are no longer carrying the pain, you are free to fill your mind with his or her good qualities. This is God's command. He knows what brings us good mental health.

Breaking Thought Patterns

THE BIBLE TELLS US TO CAST ALL OUR ANXIETIES on Jesus (1 Peter 5:7). We all try to cast our anxieties on him, but then we pick them up again and carry them ourselves. How can we keep our anxieties on Jesus? My experience in trying to break my own thought patterns can serve us as an illustration of the battle it takes to change our thought patterns and leave our anxieties with Him.

Before I left for Colombia as a missionary, I lost three members of my family in one year: my father, my mother and my brother-in-law, who left my sister alone with seven children from two to eleven years of age.

When I left to go to Costa Rica to learn Spanish, I had to sell my two most precious possessions, my car and my organ, and to say goodbye to my country. I knew that when I returned, I would have nowhere to live. My youngest sister had married and the house where the two of us had lived together after my parents' death, was now occupied by my widowed sister and her seven children. My brother's and sisters' houses were all filled with their children. There was no room for me anywhere.

In spite of this, God gave me a promise. He told me, "No one who has left home or wife or brothers or parents or children for the sake of the kingdom of God will fail to receive many times as much in this age and, in the age to come, eternal life." (Luke 18:29)

I thought, "I can understand receiving eternal life, but that you, God, will again give me father and mother and children and home in this life, that I can't understand." I felt totally alone.

I went to Costa Rica and there met Karl who would become my husband. Later we were married and went to

Colombia. Now I had a home, a husband and new parents, and soon our two children came along. In spite of this, I had a real problem. If I stayed at home when Karl traveled, I would walk from room to room praying, "Oh, God, take care of him. Please, take care of him. I don't want to lose him."

The hollow pain we had felt when my parents died would come over me again. I would relive the anguish I sensed in my sister when her husband died.

God was very kind to me. He always gave me a promise when Karl left, "I will take him safely. I will bring him safely back again."

"Lord, I believe your promise," I would pray. "But help my unbelief!" I just couldn't feel that Karl would really come back.

This continued year after year. I read all about car and bus accidents reported in the newspapers. All this terrible information accumulated in my brain. The children were growing older and began to sense my anguish.

One day, while we were living in Pasto, Karl had to travel to Tumaco to officiate some baptisms. The road from Pasto to Tumaco, which at that time was still unpaved, dropped down from high up in the Andes to the coastal plain. At one place it passed over the "Nariz del Diablo" ("The Devil's Nose"). There the narrow, unpaved road twisted along the upper edge of a 1000-foot chasm without any guardrails. Only one pointed rock at the sharpest turn provided any protection. Many buses had gone over the edge at this dangerous place. I prayed and prayed that God would send us enough money to buy a plane ticket. But no money came, and Karl had to leave by bus.

Before he left we prayed for God's protection. Again God gave me a promise, "I will take him safely. I will bless him there and will bring him safely home. Don't worry."

Karl left and I began my routine of walking from room to room, wringing my hands, and praying, "Oh, Lord! I do believe that promise… I really do… only, help my unbelief!"

That day God stopped me and said to me, "Arline, I have promised that I will take Karl safely, that I will bless him and bring him back safely. You can choose whether you are going to believe it or not believe it. On my part, I have promised and I will fulfill my promise, whether you believe it or not. You can choose what you will do. You can choose to believe me and be quiet and confident, or you can choose to keep on as you are, and teach your children that they can't trust me. The decision is yours."

I had always thought of faith as something that came over a person, something like a big, powerful, fluffy cloud; something that one didn't have before and then suddenly had. When this happened, one had no more problems with trusting God.

God taught me that day that faith was a decision I had to make. I had to accept God's promise more than what I could feel it to be true. He showed me that faith was simply deciding to trust more in His promise than in my own feelings.

That day I decided to throw all my anxieties on Jesus. "Lord Jesus, I choose to believe; this is my decision. I choose to accept your promise that Karl will come back. It is true that I cannot feel your promise. I feel that he will die and leave me alone with two little children. But you have given me a promise and I, here and now, choose to accept your promise and to believe you more than what I can feel them. I throw all these feelings and anxieties on you."

Suddenly I felt so relaxed, so free, so relieved, . . . for five minutes! After five minutes all those horrible thoughts and feelings returned in full force.

Again I prayed, "Jesus, I choose to believe your promise more than what I feel them. I throw all these anxieties on you."

Again I felt free and relaxed for about another five minutes, then all the feelings came back again. All day long I had to keep casting those anxieties on the Lord. By evening I could remain quiet for ten to fifteen minutes. The next morning I had to continue the fight. I was struggling with a nasty thought pattern. By the time Karl came back I had progressed to a point where I could remain quiet for almost twenty minutes. He returned as happy as could be because of the baptisms he had officiated.

But God still had more to teach me. The following day we read in the newspaper that the airplane, on the flight about which I had prayed so hard for a ticket, had crashed and everyone on board had perished. God had not answered my prayer in the way that I had thought He should, but He had given me the deep desire of my heart for Karl's protection.

In spite of this, my fight to break my thought habits did not end there. It was only after three or four years of casting my fears on the Lord that I could finally be quiet when Karl was traveling.

Several years later, God showed me that He had really healed me when Karl was in a car accident in Germany. Karl was hospitalized with a brain concussion, and could have been killed. I had to tell our children what happened. Through all this I remained emotionally quiet.

Several weeks later I related this experience while Karl was present.

When we were alone he exclaimed, "So, that's why you were so composed! You were so quiet it looked as though you didn't even care about the accident!" God had really healed me.

God can change your way of thinking. He changed mine even though it had become so deeply rooted. He has carried your traumas, now allow Him to change your thought patterns.

Our Natural Habitat

MANY TIMES WE ASK OURSELVES, "IF GOD loves me so much why doesn't He take me out of this problem? Why doesn't He take me out of this trial? Why do I have to go through so many temptations? Why doesn't He do something?!"

God made us with the intention that we should live in paradise. His first plan was that you and I should live in an atmosphere where everything is joy, love, contentment, understanding, companionship, and much more. He gave us the inner capacity to live and develop in that atmosphere. He never planned that we live in the atmosphere of this world as we know it now; filled with fighting, quarrels, catastrophes, and tragedies. Deep inside of ourselves, we know this and long for such a place and for such relationships.

As human beings, however, we chose not to stay there. The human race fell into sin. We no longer live in our natural psychological surroundings. God made the birds with the capacity to live in trees. He made the fish with the capacity to live in water. But we are like birds living in water or fish living in trees. We have no capacity to live in the kind of world in which we are living. Is it surprising then if we suffer from depression, anxiety, high blood pressure and ulcers?

If a bird is to live in the water, it will need a bit of air around itself to stay alive. If a fish is to live in a tree or in our house, it needs a bowl of water around itself. If we as humans are to remain well and healthy, we need a bit of paradise inside of ourselves where an atmosphere of peace and love reigns.

God could have washed His hands of us and said, "You got yourselves into this mess, now see how you get yourselves out of it!" But He didn't. God came to us in Jesus and rescued us. Jesus has promised that He will return and restore us to our own natural habitat. Some day He will take away all evil.

In the meantime, while we live between the time of the cross (our redemption) and the restoration of all things, God has not left us alone. Jesus comes to our side to carry our burdens, our pain, our traumas, our worries, in order to give us that bit of paradise inside ourselves that we so desperately need. God is more unhappy about our condition than we can ever be. He did not want us to suffer like this. If this is so, what should our attitude be when we are faced with troubles and trials? How can we comfort those who suffer?

Comforting Others

WHEN WE PASS THROUGH DIFFICULT TIMES we use many sayings to comfort each other. We say, "Be patient." We need to be patient, but we don't say how to find patience. We say, "Have faith." But what is faith? We say, "Pray." But the person has prayed and nothing has happened. We say, "Give thanks for everything." But God says (1 Thess.5:18), "Give thanks in everything." Giving thanks for every circumstance and giving thanks in every circumstance are very different.

I was giving this seminar when the father of one of my students was killed. His brother-in-law, while high on drugs, stabbed him in the abdomen and he died.

"What are we going to tell John?" I asked the students. "Should he thank God for everything? Should he thank God that his brother-in-law killed his father and left his six little brothers and sisters fatherless?" How terrible this would have been! Yet, sometimes this is actually what is said in order to "comfort" a fellow Christian.

Josephine

JOSEPHINE HAD SEVERAL SMALL CHILDREN when her husband was killed. At the funeral she cried, "God, what you have done to me is not right! What am I going to do with these children? How am I going to feed them? How can I educate them? You are unjust, God!"

Her friends hurried to console her. "Hush," they told her, "you must never say such things to God. God is never unjust. You must thank God for every circumstance. Thank God that your husband could die and is now happy with the Lord."

They made Josephine thank God that her husband could die and go to heaven. Three months later she entered a mental hospital with a complete breakdown.

Jesus never did anything like this. Even though He knew that He would raise Lazarus back to life within the next few minutes, Jesus did not scold Mary and Martha for showing their grief. He did not say, "Thank God that Lazarus could die." Jesus entered into their grief and wept with them.

How could Josephine have given thanks in her painful situation? Giving thanks for everything is so different from giving thanks in every situation. She could have continued crying out to God, "God, it isn't right what you are doing to me. What you've done is unjust! How can I provide for my children?"

She could have cried this with all the pain and bewilderment in her heart. Those who were consoling her could have encouraged her by saying, "Yes, that is true. This really feels as though God were being unjust. You feel that He is unjust. Tell Him all the pain and confusion that you feel. Cry it all out!"

Josephine could have continued crying out, "God, I don't know what you are trying to do with me. My situation looks completely impossible and hopeless! I don't understand what is going to happen. I can't believe that you can even take care of us. I don't have any faith left at all, Lord God. You said we should have the faith of God. I don't have that faith, God, but I choose to open my self up to you so that you can put your faith into me.

"God, even though I can't see or feel you, I choose to thank you that you are still my Father and are in charge of my situation. I choose to thank you that you have promised that you will not leave me alone, even though I feel that you have abandoned me. I choose to accept that even though I can see no way out of this situation, you will find a way out for me. I choose to accept, even though to me everything looks impossible, that you will somehow provide for us."

In this way Josephine could have expressed all her pain and confusion and thanked God in every situation, and her faith in Him would have been strengthened at the same time. After time had passed, she could have looked back and thanked Him for having experienced his love and provision in the midst of her trial.

We should never tell someone not to express his or her pain. Jesus wept with those who wept and we must do the same.

Another I we often use to comfort others is, "Look at your neighbor, or my friend. Her situation is much worse than yours. You don't really have a big problem. Be strong and stop complaining."

This doesn't help anyone. When we are in the middle of a trial our sky seems covered with clouds of problems from horizon to horizon. We can see no way of escape. Knowing that someone else's situation is worse than their own does not make anyone's problems feel better. It only makes people feel guilty for thinking that they have difficulties, and piles the weight of the other person's problems on top of their own. Instead of helping them, we have now burdened them down with another set of problems.

When someone is under a cloud-covered sky it is impossible to tell how thick the clouds are. The thickness of the cloud layer can only be seen from an airplane. One person's sky may be covered with a very thick layer of clouds while another person's is covered with a thin layer, but both of their skies are covered from horizon to horizon. Neither of them can see a way out. We only intensify people's pain and thicken their cloud layer when we heap on them the guilt of not thinking about other people's problems.

Sometimes we try to comfort others by saying, "Don't worry, God is only testing you to see how strong you are."

One evening when we were ready to begin a meeting in our church in Colombia, we were told that the house of one of the members had burned to the ground. They had escaped with only the clothes they were wearing.

Liliana accompanied me to their neighbors' house, where the family had found refuge, in order to comfort them. As we entered the house, Liliana rushed to them and said hurriedly, "This is just God's way of trying to see if you love Him. Don't worry, it is only a trial to see how strong you are! He just wants to see if you love Him more than your material things! It's only a test. If you pass the test He'll know that you love Him . . . ."

The poor woman who had lost everything stood there bewildered and confused. Liliana's "comforting" words had only added to her pain and confusion. When I managed to get close and opened my arms to her, she put her head on my shoulder and cried and cried. That was what she needed. She needed another way to express her pain. We took them to our home to eat and later found clothing and a place for them to stay.

Was Liliana right in saying that God sends us trials in order to see if we really love Him? We will examine this question more closely in the next chapter.

CHAPTER 10

A Life Ready for Service

WHY MUST WE SUFFER TRIALS and temptations? What is God trying to do with us? Does God really send trials and temptations just to see if we are strong enough to withstand them? In 1 Corinthians 10:13 we are told:

No temptation has seized you except what is common to man. And God is faithful; He will not let you be tempted beyond what you can bear. But when you are tempted, He will also provide a way out so that you can stand up under it.

This verse does not say, "and God is faithful; He will only allow you to be tempted in order to see how much you are able to bear."

God already knows how strong we are. Doesn't He know everything? Does He need to prove us in order to learn how much we can take? Of course not! The problem is that we ourselves don't know how strong we have grown in Him.

In Job 1:10, Satan appeared before God. God asked him, "Have you seen my servant Job? He's a very good man."

Satan answered, "Have you not put a hedge around him and his household and everything he has?"

Satan wanted to tempt Job and make him curse God. He hurled all kinds of temptations and trials at Job, all to no avail. Every time Satan tried to get near him, he ran into God's hedge. Satan simply couldn't get at Job.

Job wanted to serve God with all his heart (chapter 1). Although he was walking in the center of God's will, he must have been afraid of losing his family, his health and his possessions (chapter 3:25). Until that time God had totally protected him and everything he owned. We could illustrate this in the following way:

<Insert Image 14>

Satan said, in effect, "Of course Job serves you! You don't let me do a thing against him. You don't even let me touch him!"

God answered, in essence, "Okay, I'll make a hole in the hedge. Everything that he has is in your hands. But don't you lay a finger on Job himself!"

God knew how strong Job had grown and measured exactly the trial that He permitted. Satan was allowed to destroy everything Job owned but he could not touch Job's person. We could illustrate this in the following way:

<Insert Image 15>

Later Satan again appeared before God. "Look at what you have done to my servant Job, and he hasn't even sinned," God said to him.

"Skin for skin; a man will give everything he has for his life," Satan replied. (Job 2:4)

"Okay," said God, "he's in your hands, but don't take away his life."

God knew Job had grown stronger during the first attack and made another hole in the hedge around him. Satan could now touch his body but not take his life. This new trial was measured exactly to fit Job's strength. This can be illustrated in the following way:

<Insert Image 16>

Possibly if Satan had been permitted to touch Job's body the first time, the trial would have been more than Job could bear. God knew exactly how strong he had grown. It is very clear that Satan's intention was to destroy Job, but God had another purpose in mind. As long as Job was living in God's will, absolutely nothing could touch him but that which God permitted in order to reach that purpose.

The same holds true for us. As long as we are living in God's will and plan we are totally safe. Nothing can touch us that cannot be used in order to serve God's purpose for our lives. But woe unto us if we should be found outside of his will and protection!

Satan can then reach us with any trial or temptation with which he desires. His purpose is to destroy us. If we are outside of God's protection, it may be that we really cannot resist his attacks. In our own strength, we are like ships in the wind tossed about to and fro, without an anchor. This can be shown with the following illustration:

<Insert Image 17>

As long as we are living in God's will, the very fact that we find ourselves in some trial or temptation already tells us that we are able to bear it. God would not have permitted that trial if we had not had the strength to resist.

1 Corinthians 10:13 tells us that God is faithful. He will not permit us to be tempted above what we are able to bear. He will, together with the temptation, give us a way of escape. The problem is that when we are in a trial or temptation, we are often so busy crying out to God to get us out of our problems that we forget to ask Him to show us the way of escape. God always provides an escape, but Satan tries to hide the way of escape so cleverly that we can't find it.

Many times we pray, "God, take me out of this trial! Take away this temptation!" But James 1:2,12,17 reads:

Count it all joy, my brothers, when you face trials of many kinds.... Blessed is the man who perseveres under trial, because when he has stood the test he will receive the crown of life... Every good and perfect gift is from above, coming down from the Father of heavenly lights, who does not change like shifting shadows.

God tells us that if we find ourselves in trials we should accept them with joy. This is exactly the opposite of what we do. When we say, "God, take away this trial," according to verse twelve we are actually saying, "God, I don't care about that crown you want to give me. I just want to live peacefully now. I don't care what happens later!" Only when we have endured the trial will we receive the crown of life. Which is more important: to have the crown of life for all eternity or to have several hours of peace now?

What we need to cry in the midst of our trials is, "God, this trial feels as though it were entirely too big for me to bear. I can't see any way out. But you have promised that you won't allow me to be tempted above what I can bear. You promised there would always be a way out. Please put your strength into me and show me your way of escape."

My mother told me that when she needed to punish me when I was a little girl, I would run to her and grab her tightly around her knees. This put me in such close contact with her that she couldn't get enough leverage to really spank me. She needed to keep me at arm's length to make the spanking worthwhile. I didn't know this was happening. I only knew that if I could grab my mother tightly, the spankings didn't hurt so much.

When we are going through trials we tend to run away from God and the hurt increases. What we need to do is run to God, hold onto him tightly, and let Him carry our pain. Nothing can touch us that is not first measured by Him; there is always a way out.

We may ask ourselves, "But if God already knows that I'm strong enough to overcome this trial, why do I have to know that I'm that strong? Why can't I just live in peace? What is God trying to do with me?"

The Parrot

WE ARE LIKE THE WILD PARROT A HUNTER brought to his friend in the city. His friend put the parrot into a big wire cage that covered the wall of his patio. The parrot flew against the side of the cage and fell down. Again it hurled itself against the cage and fell to the floor.

Eventually the hunter told his friend to chain the parrot lest it kill itself.

So he fastened one end of the chain to the parrot's leg and the other to the wooden perch. The parrot flew to the end of the chain and fell, then tried again. When it finally realized it was chained and couldn't escape, it settled down, sat on the perch and accepted its fate.

When the hunter returned, he removed the chain because the parrot was tamed. The parrot, however, did not realize that the chain was gone. It thought it was still chained to the perch. It had accepted its plight and no longer tried to escape.

This family also had a cat. One day the children left the door of the cage open, and the cat crept into the cage. Because the parrot thought it was still chained, it continued sitting motionless on its perch and allowed the cat to sneak up, catch it and eat it up.

That cage was big enough that the parrot could have flown up, swooped out the door and saved its life. But since it thought it was still chained, it sat on the perch and allowed itself to be eaten up.

If someone had earlier poked a stick into the cage and knocked the unchained parrot to the floor, it might have cried out, "Leave me in peace! Why must you torment me? Isn't my condition bad enough? I was stolen from my home and freedom and stuck into this cage and now you're knocking me to the floor!"

But soon, in spite of its complaints, the parrot would have begun to use its wings again. It would have learned that it was free. When the cat entered the cage, it would have swooped out the door to safety.

We are like that parrot. Satan has us chained, and we have learned that we are helpless. Then God allows us to go through different experiences, each of which makes us grow a bit stronger, until He sees that we have grown strong and free from our weaknesses and failures. But we are not aware of this. We think we are still chained and unable to face difficult situations. Job had said, "That which I feared has come upon me" (Job 3:25). He had thought he couldn't live without his possessions.

Then God permits a trial or temptation that knocks us down. We cry,

"Oh, God, take this trial away from me! It's killing me! Don't I have enough problems already? Please take it away. I can't stand it!"

But God doesn't take the trial away. We cry out again, "God, why are you treating me like this? Please get me out of here!"

In spite of this, God allows the trial to continue. Little by little, in the midst of the trial, we find our "wings of faith" and begin to fly. We rise to victory by faith. When we learn that we can live victoriously right in the middle of everything, the trial soon ends.

Then we realize that we have discovered the way out to victory. We are free! When it is over, we will look back and say, "Thank you, Lord, for what you taught me through that experience. I wouldn't ever want to go through it again, but I thank you for what I learned."

In God's Private University

GOD DREW MY ATTENTION TO 2 CORINTHIANS 1:3-4 when I was going through a very, very difficult time. Seven weeks before graduating from nursing school, I received a telephone call that my mother had suffered a brain hemorrhage. She was in bed with her right side completely paralyzed, and couldn't speak. As soon as I finished school, I had to return home and help care for her. I had wanted to go to college and prepare to be a missionary. Now, I had to stay at home and, as far as I could see, vegetate for many years.

My mother was a complete invalid. My younger sister and I cared for her like a child. The only way she could communicate with us was to stick out her tongue if she meant to say "yes," and to not stick it out if she meant "no." Later she was unable to do even that. Eventually she could only breathe deeply for "yes" and breathe normally for "no." This continued for over three years.

During this time I became ill with rheumatic fever and was bedridden for six months. I wasn't even supposed to hang my feet over the edge of my bed lest my pulse increase and my heart be damaged. In spite of this, I had to get up and care for my mother at night so that my sister could sleep. It is a miracle that I don't have a damaged heart valve.

Two months after I recuperated my father suffered his first coronary infarction. He was bedfast for six weeks. A short time after my father's condition improved, we all got an Asiatic flu with a fever of over 103 F degrees and a very severe cough.

My mother had an umbilical hernia which protruded every time she coughed. We tried to tape her hernia but she was allergic to the tape and ended up with a skin burn. That meant that with my high fever, I had to stand by her bedside all night and hold in her hernia while she coughed.

Several days before we got the flu, my sister, a right-handed art student, had fallen and fractured her right arm. Now, with her high fever and fierce cough, she was in agony. In the middle of this, we discovered that my father was diabetic and needed to follow a strict diet. When we pulled out of this crisis, we had two months of quiet. Then suddenly my father had another coronary infarction and died within forty-eight hours. Nine weeks later my mother died. Six months after that I was hospitalized for emergency gallbladder surgery. Six months after that my brother-in-law was killed in a traffic accident leaving my sister alone with seven children, from two to eleven years of age. We felt like Job (23:8-10):

> But if I go to the east, He is not there; if I go to the west, I do not find Him. When He is at work in the north, I do not see Him; when He turns to the south, I catch no glimpse of Him. But He knows the way I take; when He has tested me, I will come forth as gold.

In the middle of all this pain and distress, God showed me the verses in 2 Corinthians 1:3-4:

> Praise be to God the Father of our Lord Jesus Christ, the Father of compassion, and the God of all comfort, who comforts us in all our troubles, so that we can comfort those in any trouble with the comfort we ourselves have received from God.

In the midst of our trials, God gave me His consolation. When I graduated from nursing school, I had wanted to go to college and prepare for the mission field, but God put me into His own private university at home. It was there that He consoled me and taught me these lessons that I later used to bring consolation and comfort to others.

God does not send angels to comfort us. They cannot enter into what we feel. They have never suffered our trials and pains. They cannot give us the consolation that we need. God sends people who have suffered and received his consolation, and who can pass that consolation on to others.

So what is God trying to do by allowing you to suffer those trials? He is trying to teach and console you and make you a useful instrument to minister to others, just as He was teaching Ekhart.

Ekhard

Ekhard was going blind. Several times people had prayed with him for healing, but he never got better. Then he was told that he wasn't healed because he lacked faith. But no one could tell him how to get that faith.

"I believe that God can heal me, that He wants to heal me, but how can I get that faith?" asked Ekhard.

"It is the will of God that you be blind," others told him.

"How can it be possible that God who loves me, wants me to be blind? Can you believe that it could be the will of God that I be blind for the rest of my life, and be such a burden to my wife and family?" he asked me. "I just can't believe that God, who is love, could want this. How can you explain this?"

"Ekhard," I told him, "you can know for sure that it is not God's will that you remain blind. God's original plan for your life was that you would live in paradise, where there was no sickness, no sin and no death. That was God's will for you. It is not God's will that you remain in this lamentable condition in which you are now. He is more unhappy and sorry about it than you can ever be."

I explained to Ekhard that God's original plan for us was that we live in paradise, where there is no sickness, no fighting, no misunderstanding, no death. He gave us the capacity to live in that environment. He did not give us the capacity to live in this world as we know it now. We are like birds living in water or fish living in trees. We are outside of our natural habitat. This is not God's fault. Our race chose to leave our natural environment.

But God will not leave us to our fate. According to Revelation 22, He will restore our natural environment in the New Heaven and the New Earth. Because of this, I could with all confidence assure Ekhard that God would restore his vision, either in this life by a miracle, or later, at the restoration of all things, with a new body. In the meantime, God is more unhappy over Ekhard's condition than he himself could ever be.

"During the time that you are blind, Ekhard, Jesus is at your side," I told him. "He tells you in 1 Peter 1:7 to cast all your anxieties on Him, because He cares for you. Your anxiety is being a burden to your wife and family. Another of your anxieties is needing to continually ask where things are located. Cast all these anxieties on Jesus. He wants to carry them for you. He knows you can't bear them since He didn't put that capacity into you when He made you.

"While you go through this time of adjustment and confusion, open yourself to God's consolation. When you have been comforted by God, He will send others to you who are in trials similar to the one you are in now. He will use you to bring to them the same consolation and comfort that He is giving to you now. This will make your life useful in God's kingdom in such ways and in such depth that you couldn't even know existed before this trial came to you. Like Job, Ekhard, you will come to know God in ways that you never knew Him before."

Job had prayed and searched after God (chapter 1). He had wanted to know God, to come closer to Him. At the end of his long trial, he said (42:5), "My ears had heard of you, but now my eyes have seen you."

The whole book of Job relates the story of his difficulties and trials and the way his friends tried to comfort him. Finally Job came through to the other side of his trials and God restored double everything Satan had destroyed. Job now knew God so much better. Before, he had only heard of God; now, he saw Him. God's purpose through all of Job's trials was that Job should come to know Him better and in a more personal way–exactly what Job himself had been longing for in the first chapter of his story. Job had learned what God wanted to teach him.

The School of God

Life can be compared to a school. During the year many things are learned, and then comes the exam. If we pass the test we go on to learn something new. If we fail, we must go back and take the course again. Job passed the test. He did not need to go through the same trial again. He was ready to go on to new things. When you are going through a trial (the exam) it seems as though it would never end, as though for the rest of your life you would go on being tested in the same way. But there is an end. When you have learned what God wants to teach you, the end of the trial will come and you will go on to new things. Then you can look back and thank God for what you learned.

I couldn't thank God for my years of suffering when I was experiencing them. But now, looking back, I thank Him for what I suffered. I wouldn't want to go through it again, but I thank Him for everything that I learned. Because I suffered and was consoled and comforted, I can understand, console and comfort others who are suffering.

If we want lives that are useful to God, we must not flee from our trials, because He has a purpose for allowing them. As long as you remain in the will of God, you can be completely sure that no matter in what problem, trial or difficulty you may find yourself, it has been measured exactly according to the strength that you have in Jesus. Through your suffering you will learn to know this strength, you will receive the consolation of God, and you will become an instrument in God's hands to bring his comfort to others.

As with Job, the enemy intends to use these temptations and trials to destroy you. He has brought all the past traumas into your life with the full intention of destroying you and making you unusable. But the beauty of it all is that God takes precisely that incident, that trial, that temptation that caused you so much pain and difficulty, heals and consoles you, and then uses it to make you usable to reach others. In other words, what God uses to make you usable is exactly that which Satan intended to use to destroy you. Isn't this what you want? Don't you want God to use you to bring healing and consolation to others? You are receiving God's healing, consolation and comfort. You are now ready to go out and carry this healing to others. Take a few moments right now to thank God for what He is doing in your life.

ABOUT THE AUTHOR

ARLINE (MAUST) WESTMEIER is an international, speaker, author and counselor who has helped men and women around the globe find healing for their past hurts. A registered nurse, certified Christian Counselor and Traumatologist, she holds undergraduate and graduate degrees in Bible, Psychology and Theology and a doctorate in Psychology and Religion (Drew University, Madison, NJ).

She was born in the Allegheny Mountains near Meyersdale, Pennsylvania, and lived there until leaving for the mission field. Together with her late husband, Karl W Westmeier, from Flechtdorf, Germany, she served as a missionary in Colombia, South America, and Puerto Rico for 38 years. She has presented seminars on healing and counseling in the United States, Europe, Africa, Central and South America. She is the mother of an adult son and daughter, and has two adolescent grandsons. Since the death of her beloved husband in April, 2018, she is living in Grantsville, Md. in the beautiful Alleghany Mountains.

Healing the Wounded Soul is a four-volume set.

Ways to Inner Wholeness is the first volume. Although each volume addresses healing in a specific area of life, they can also be read separately. This book was first published in Spanish, German and Croation.

www.ingramcontent.com/pod-product-compliance
Lightning Source LLC
LaVergne TN
LVHW011946070526
838202LV00054B/4814